saving you

Also by Charlotte Nash

Ryders Ridge
Iron Junction
Crystal Creek
The Horseman
The Paris Wedding

Charlotte Nash

saving you

hachette
AUSTRALIA

hachette
AUSTRALIA

Published in Australia and New Zealand in 2019
by Hachette Australia
(an imprint of Hachette Australia Pty Limited)
Level 17, 207 Kent Street, Sydney NSW 2000
www.hachette.com.au

10 9 8 7 6 5 4 3 2 1

Copyright © Charlotte Nash 2019

A catalogue record for this
book is available from the
National Library of Australia

ISBN: 978 0 7336 3647 9

Cover design by Christabella Designs
Cover images courtesy of Shutterstock
Author photo courtesy of Jen Dainer, Industrial Arc Photography
Typeset in 12/17 pt Sabon LT Pro by Bookhouse, Sydney
Printed and bound in Australia by McPherson's Printing Group

MIX
Paper from
responsible sources
FSC® C001695

The paper this book is printed on is certified against the
Forest Stewardship Council® Standards. McPherson's Printing
Group holds FSC® chain of custody certification SA-COC-005379.
FSC® promotes environmentally responsible, socially beneficial
and economically viable management of the world's forests.

For Vic, who keeps my faith in the goodness and kindness of people's hearts

Chapter 1

MALLORY COOK HAD LIVED IN THE LITTLE GREEN COTTAGE since the day she'd left school, seven long years ago. She and Duncan had taken it because of the extremely low rent, and because after being rejected from several other prospects, they were rather desperate to find a place to live. It was the cottage or couch surfing, and standing at the end of the long drive, the cottage seemed the better choice.

From a distance, the place had certainly looked like a colonial postcard: all cosy beneath the trees, with a distinguished gable, a wide brick chimney, and an outhouse of firewood promising comfort on cold winter nights. Up close, though, even an enthusiastic real estate agent would have had trouble ignoring the lean in the floors, the hideous mould problem, and the cracks and holes that let in all the spiders. The curtains were so thin that they lit up like ghosts in storms, and the location on an old avocado farm meant they were far from potentially helpful neighbours. But these features had never bothered Mallory.

Only two things really bothered her. The first was the black-cloud storms that thundered in off the sea and collected the cottage in a full-frontal assault every few days in the summer. One of those storms had lashed the windows last night, even though it was autumn already.

The second was the fact that a year ago, Duncan had suddenly moved his fledgling company all the way to New York, leaving his fledgling family – Mallory and their five-year-old son, Harry – to manage on their own. They'd grown apart anyway, he'd said, which was news to Mallory. The shock had been just like one of those storms, only it had taken much longer than a night to blow itself out.

Despite storms and absent husbands, when Mallory woke on this particular Friday morning, she knew today would be the best day of her life.

She danced to the radio as she pulled the limp doona up to make the bed, removing a large bear from under the covers. It belonged to Harry, and she'd taken it with her for comfort last night. But she wouldn't need it again after today. By the time midnight came, her little boy would be back across the hall, tucked in the red racing-car bed they'd painted together. Duncan would be sitting on the lime-green sofa, the one they'd recovered from a skip bin when they were first married. They'd laughed so much that day, delirious with the delight of moving into the cottage, even though Duncan's computer desk had to be made from planks and milk crates. Mallory crossed her fingers, deep in full-fantasy imagining: Duncan would laugh when she reminded him of the sofa's origins. Then she would tell him about her new promotion, showing him he wasn't the only one who could make it. They would talk into the late hours while Harry slept, mending whatever it was that had gone wrong to make Duncan move halfway across the world.

After all, the signs were good. He had finally paid for Harry to visit him in New York, which must mean that the business had stabilised. The round-the-clock stress of being a newly successful CEO, which had made Duncan unavailable so often this past year, appeared to be over. The two of them were flying back today, and Duncan had said that he wanted to 'talk'. Mallory had heard all kinds of apology and hope in his voice. They could work everything out.

Mallory held on to that thought as she shook out her blue work uniform and mixed her first instant coffee of the day. She drank it at the kitchen window, looking out on the chickens scratching about in the grass. Water drops hung like jewels on the shaggy jasmine around the window; it was always in need of a prune. The tiny kitchen, however, was unusually immaculate. The tiled benchtops wiped, all the water spots removed from the single sink, Harry's pictures arranged to cover the rusting cracks on the fridge, and the wonky cabinet door coaxed into a straight alignment. Mallory had enjoyed the temporary calm of her boy being away, but she missed the signs of Harry being home: the half-finished bowl of Weet-Bix on the sink, the drawing pencils and paper on the bench, his favourite blue vinyl chair always pulled out. The house was too empty without him.

She rinsed her cup and checked her diary, supressing the nerves that sprang from reading 'job interview' scrawled across one o'clock. She normally rated job interviews somewhere between the spiders that lurked in the shower and the thunderstorms. And while she was tired of dealing with both of those on her own, the interview was something she could handle. She wasn't even worried about freezing up with nerves, or launching into some awful verbal diarrhoea.

Today, her boys were coming home and everything was right with the world.

The morning seemed full of good omens. Her ancient Corolla started on the first try, and she caught every green light into work.

Her workplace, the Silky Oaks Residential Care Facility, sat on a hilltop looking down on Moreton Bay, its double-storey edifice rising from beautifully kept gardens, with a stand of wild and untamed eucalypts kept at a safe distance beyond the southern boundary. Mallory waved to a gardener who was busy clearing fallen branches, no doubt casualties of the storm, and paused to appreciate the view of two white-sailed yachts out on the sparkling water. Unlike her cottage, everything close up matched the postcard beauty of that view. Silky Oaks boasted white walls, tasteful art, and a gentle smell of lavender and rose petals. And if it was a little too bright and clinical for Mallory at times, the place was certainly organised, clean and efficient. It couldn't have run any other way with Mrs Crawley, Director, at the helm – the same person whom Mallory would face at her job interview.

Mallory wasn't that worried because Mrs Crawley knew her. Mallory had worked at the Silky Oaks Care Facility almost as long as she'd lived in her cottage, seven dedicated years as a staff carer. She was one of the very few veterans, and had seen many other staff come and go. Now, a position had opened for an Engagement Manager, and Mallory wanted it more than anything in the world, beyond having Harry and Duncan back.

She stowed her bag in the staffroom and jogged into the nearest ground-floor resident's room, humming the same boppy pop song. Then she went to work transferring her residents down to the breakfast tables, and chatting with them about the day ahead.

'The kindergarten class is coming at eleven,' she told Evelyn, and Sue, and Mr Burgundy, who'd been a music teacher and still insisted on being called 'Mr'. But his smile was the broadest when he heard the class was coming. Mallory loved these moments with her residents. It was the whole reason she did this job. She was humming again by the time she returned to help strip beds.

'You're in a good mood. What's that you're singing?' asked Bridget in her broad Scottish accent. She was Mallory's closest work friend, serial pusher of baked goods, and occasional font of motherly advice.

'Just the last thing I heard on the radio this morning.'

Bridget laughed. 'I thought you'd still be turning inside out with nerves, after the storm last night. I nearly rang you up to make sure you weren't under the bed.'

'I was fine,' Mallory lied, glossing over the hour of clutching Harry's bear so hard that she'd had fur under her fingernails. She checked her watch; her interview was hours away, but her stomach still flipped.

'I'm sure you'll do well,' Bridget said, when Mallory admitted her nerves.

'What's the worst that can happen, right?'

Bridget shook her head. 'I don't like to think like that, but no one deserves it more. Lord knows you're braver than me. Crawley scares me witless.'

•

Bridget's statement had the unfortunate effect of priming Mallory to notice the intimidating side of Mrs Crawley. By the time the administrative assistant showed Mallory into Mrs Crawley's office, Mallory's stomach had a full crew of tap-dancing butterflies on high alert. The office was neat and tastefully appointed, with plush red chairs, soft tan carpet, and a framed modern art print on the wall. A large window faced out into the garden with a glimpse of the water. For families and relatives, it was probably soothing and orderly. Mallory simply felt out of place.

Mrs Crawley sat reading a letter, her back to the window. She wore a dove-grey suit and black-rimmed glasses. A minimally applied coral lipstick was the only brightness in her face, the skin around her mouth smooth from being a career non-smiler. The air smelled of vanilla, which normally reminded Mallory of Bridget's home baking, but today seemed to reek of foreboding. Mallory tried to sit up straight and not fidget but she could feel her heart crashing around in her ribs, and the cramp developing between her shoulderblades. Finally, Mrs Crawley briskly signed the letter and filed it in her out-tray. She removed her glasses.

'Mallory. Well. Thank you for your interest in this role.'

'Of course,' Mallory said, her tongue so thick she had to force the words out. 'It's just such a dream job. I was really excited to see it come up. You see, ever since I started working here I've wanted to, and I just thought, yes . . .'

She trailed off, aware she was doing the verbal diarrhoea thing. Mrs Crawley was staring at her. Mallory clamped her lips shut and smiled.

After a small pause, Mrs Crawley picked up a sheaf of papers and said, 'Yes, well, your application was certainly thorough. I think it might be useful if I talk a little bit about this position, and what we need from the applicant.'

Mallory sat forward, eager to move on. At eighteen, she'd come needing a job, but Silky Oaks was now her second home. She knew every inch of its white walls and lino floors, and all about the lives of the residents on her roster. She knew the number of seconds it took to get hot water in the tap in each bathroom, and how to pound the third locker in the staffroom when it stuck. She wanted to step up.

'The Engagement Manager is responsible for all the activity programs we run within Silky Oaks for all the residents, including weekly, monthly and special events. That's everything from craft, to film screenings, to group visits like the community choir. It's across both floors and four wings. We need someone who can coordinate a large number of people's needs and resources within a strict budget, and follow through in an orderly way. The residents' lives need routine.'

Mrs Crawley paused. So far, all this had been on the job description. Mallory didn't exactly agree with everything Mrs Crawley had said, but she knew she could do this job.

'Yes, I understand,' she said. 'Because I'm really very passionate about Silky Oaks and the people who live here. I've loved the changes I've helped make and I think I can continue to do that as the Engagement Manager.'

'Good, good, that's all good. You have a lot of enthusiasm.' Mrs Crawley gave Mallory a smile, but it was a careful smile, one that said she didn't quite mean the praise she was offering. Mallory's stomach dipped.

'I have more ideas than what I put in my application,' she rushed on, needing Mrs Crawley to believe she was serious. 'I've managed a tight budget, and I have good relationships with all the elders.'

'We prefer "resident" here,' Mrs Crawley corrected.

'Of course. Sorry. I mean, I'm good with people.'

Though Mallory wasn't quite sure that Mrs Crawley fell into the group of people she was good with. She tried a warm smile, which was usually a safe fallback move. Mrs Crawley merely lifted the bridge of her glasses and rubbed at her nose, as if all this smiling had given her allergies.

'Tell me more about your ideas,' she said as she replaced the glasses.

'Well,' Mallory began, 'I know that many residents are lonely. That was one of the reasons I proposed the kindergarten class.'

Lonely was sometimes an understatement. It happened so often that families began by visiting regularly, but then life took over and those visits dropped away, leaving mothers and fathers and grandparents separated from the people who had defined their life. It broke Mallory's heart. A year ago, in the wake of Duncan's departure, she'd approached Harry's kindergarten teacher and proposed that the class visit Silky Oaks each week. She thought it would be easy, since the kindergarten was just over the hill and behind the trees from Silky Oaks: the very reason Mallory had chosen it. The weeks of negotiations that followed left her sleepless and jittery. But while weekly visits had to become fortnightly, and outdoor activities were abandoned for story time in the lounge, the program was still an unqualified hit. The residents loved it, and so did the children. The residents told fascinating stories, and the children were delightfully spontaneous and unpredictable.

'But I want to take the idea further,' Mallory said. 'The class can't be here every day, and I think many of the eld— residents would love that connection and companionship more of the time.'

'So you're proposing pets.'

Mallory paused, seeing the twitch at the corner of Mrs Crawley's mouth. 'It's been done in some other care facilities, and they have seen these amazing increases in happiness and even less medication. I really think—'

'Yes, I see.' Mrs Crawley clasped her hands together on her desk. 'The thing is, Mallory, this is a management position. And managers have many considerations to make. The kindergarten class has been an interesting pilot program, but it has come at a price, one that I'm not sure you've quite understood.'

Mallory sat absolutely still, feeling small and vulnerable, as though she'd landed in the principal's office. She knew Silky Oaks hadn't been wild about the class visits at first, but she'd thought the success had swept those reservations away.

'The administrative load is very high. All the residents had to have Blue Cards. We had to check insurance and liability, and then there was the guinea pig incident.'

Even under pressure, Mallory had to purse her lips to avoid laughing. A few months ago one of the children had smuggled a guinea pig into Silky Oaks. Bridget had been the one who discovered three children introducing the animal to Mr Burgundy. The children had been teaching Mr Burgundy about the guinea pig, and Mr Burgundy had been suggesting composer-themed names, like Mozart and Brahms, and humming rousing bars from symphony scores.

Mallory had been shown the whole thing on the security tape, and she had been delighted because Mr Burgundy was often so quiet. Just watching him open up over the tiny furry visitor had prompted her thinking about pets to start with. Evidently, Mrs Crawley had neither been fascinated nor delighted.

'I know we had a few problems,' Mallory said carefully. 'But we'll learn from that. And anything that improves the lives of the residents has to be a good thing. Craft is great, but it can't give you that sense that someone else understands you and loves you. I think having animals here could do such amazing things. Even if it was chickens – they could be outside. And a garden – then we could have eggs and vegetables for cooking, really involve everyone in our community. Of course, I'll make a proper plan with all the research supporting it.' She rushed out the last sentence, aware her earnest words were failing to move Mrs Crawley.

'I'm sure you would.' Mrs Crawley gave her another, not unkind smile. 'But that's not the only issue. In a management position, the hours are more regular, but longer. The work schedule can be tough if you don't have much . . . family support to share the load.'

The pause told Mallory that Mrs Crawley really *did* know everything.

Mallory swallowed. 'My husband's just been in New York while his business was setting up,' she said, tweaking the truth. 'He's coming back. Today, in fact.'

'Really? I see.'

A long pause settled, during which the automatic scent dispenser on the wall puffed out a fresh shot of vanilla. Mallory suppressed a sneeze, which nearly turned into tears. It dawned on her that this promotion was not only *not* going to be hers, but that she had probably never been a serious contender.

'Look, Mallory, I will be honest with you. You're a hard worker, and that's something I value. But you're young. Most of the people we interview for this position have university qualifications. I'd like to see you gain some more experience, perhaps we could even help with some courses, and then apply again in another couple of years. When you have a much better grasp of the role. All right?'

Mrs Crawley squared the pages and slotted them into her out-tray.

And that was the end of Mallory's first hope.

•

Bridget found Mallory splashing water on her blotched face in the staff locker room.

'I take it that didn't go well,' Bridget said. Then, when Mallory turned to face her, 'Lord above! What on earth did she say? You look like you've been crying all morning.'

Mallory pressed the damp towel to her cheeks. 'I just blush like this. Mum used to think I'd been sunburned. I was hoping to look less fluorescent before I go back out there.' She sighed. 'And no. She's looking for someone older, and more . . . managerial, I suppose. But she did say she liked my enthusiasm,' Mallory added, trying to find a way to lessen the humiliation. She hung the towel. 'Do you think she might change her mind, if they don't find another candidate?'

Bridget popped an eyebrow. 'I suppose there's chilly nights in hell.'

Mallory winced, deeply wounded. Not just because she really hadn't been in the running for the job, but also that her ideas wouldn't find a ready welcome. How could she keep working here if she couldn't promise better days ahead for her residents? She pulled open her locker, where a series of Harry photos lined the door.

'I'm so sorry, Mal,' Bridget was saying. 'I know how much you wanted this, and you'd have been wonderful. I have no doubts.'

'At least Harry's coming back tonight,' Mallory said, staring at the photo of him holding his bantam chicken in the cottage's backyard, eyes scrunched: his standard response to being asked to smile. She touched the photo, wishing her love to him.

'Wait a minute.'

'Mmm?' Mallory turned to find Bridget with her hands on her ample hips, peering at Mallory's locker.

Bridget pointed a finger. 'What is that?'

Mallory knew exactly what Bridget had seen. The dress was hardly unnoticeable. Blood red, it was covered in delicate embroidered gold flowers. Mallory had worn it to her senior formal, her first date with Duncan. Duncan had said he loved it, loved the way she'd worn the bold colour and short skirt among a crowd of slinky black floor-length numbers. Mallory had kept it in plastic in the back of her cupboard ever since. She'd been seventeen, and it still fit.

She shrugged. 'I'm going straight to the airport after work. I wanted to get changed.'

'Into that?'

'I wanted to look nice,' Mallory said, hoping nonchalance would fool Bridget's Scottish intuition. That it wouldn't be obvious that Mallory was only wearing the dress because of Duncan.

Bridget heaved a sigh and gave Mallory a kind pat on her shoulder. 'Please tell me you're not doing what I think you're doing. You're not thinking of taking him back?'

Mallory closed the locker. 'He wants to talk. I have to give him that,' she said, trying to suppress her hopes of far more than *just talking*.

'Do you really think that's a good idea? I'm not judging, mind. I just care about you. I don't want to see you so hurt again.'

'He's still my husband, and Harry's father,' Mallory said. 'Here, look.'

She pulled a letter out of her pocket. It had arrived two days ago and was already creased from handling. Bridget unfolded the letter, full of Harry's large, childish letters, and a drawing with three stick figures labelled 'Mum', 'Dad' and 'me'. Next was a printed photo: Duncan and Harry together, identical grins on their faces, the same little ruffle at the end of their left eyebrows, holding a homemade sign that read, *Wish You Were Here*. The New York Aquarium was behind them.

Bridget sighed, and slipped Mallory's justifications of love and forgiveness back into the envelope. 'I suppose,' she said doubtfully.

'And he says his company is doing really well. It wouldn't be like before,' Mallory said.

'You mean, like when you were struggling to feed all three of you while he sat at home tinkering with his computer? What would you do, move to New York?'

Mallory hesitated. She hadn't even thought about the details. All she'd wanted was time to talk with Duncan, without the pressures that had been around them a year ago, when his company was taking off. She was certain that if they could just spend some time together, they could work it out. She didn't like Bridget's doubt.

'We haven't settled any details,' Mallory said. 'But I don't want to be that person who couldn't give him another chance. I know you think he bummed off me until he didn't need me anymore, but it wasn't that simple. He was under such pressure. Look at how many people here don't have their families anymore, Bridge. I want mine back.'

Bridget sighed. 'Aye, I understand that. Good luck to you, then. And you'd better wish me luck, too. One of the ladies I'm taking down to the lunch room next took a swing at me last time. I think she didn't like my jokes.'

'Good luck,' Mallory called, sneaking another look at the photos in her locker before she headed back to work.

Once lunch was over and her residents resettled in their rooms for an afternoon rest, Mallory was rostered to cleaning duty in the south wing: a tidiness and cleanliness check of the family lounge, computer room, and small TV room. Mallory moved through the lounge, straightening chairs, re-sticking Blu Tack on the Easter drawings the children had made two weeks ago, and trying not to dwell on the lost promotion. She listened to the news headlines while she changed the bins in the TV room: Trump had tweeted something outrageous again, a volcano somewhere in the Pacific north-west was threatening to erupt, a footballer had won some kind of medal. She shut off the TV.

In the computer room, she tucked the chair into the desk, turned off the monitor and collected a page left in the printer tray. She was on her way to the paper bin when she noticed it was an airline itinerary.

Brisbane to Los Angeles, then Los Angeles to Nashville, it said. That was a big trip. She knew many of the people who lived at Silky Oaks, but she didn't recognise the name at the top: Ernest Flint.

'Is Ernest Flint in this wing?' she asked the nurse who was eating lunch at the desk across the hall. 'I think he might have left something in the computer room.'

The woman made a face. 'Ernie hasn't used a computer in his life. Jock's the only one who's been in there today. Room twenty-six on the second floor.'

Mallory found the door to room twenty-six open, and immediately glimpsed a resident with a difference. The room might have held the same furniture as all the others – the king single bed on one wall made up in a plain blue quilt, a desk under the window. But the opposite long wall had been painted a deep navy, and supported a bookshelf, crammed with books and models and jam jars filled with miniature brushes. More hand-painted military plane and helicopter models hung from the ceiling on fishing line. Jock himself sat at the desk, ringed with neat piles of logic problem books, his pencil poised above a crossword. He was short and wiry, and wearing a worn green fishing hat covered in badges. Under the back, Mallory glimpsed clipped grey hair.

She knocked, and the eyes that swung around were bright blue and wary.

'Hello,' she said. 'We haven't met. I'm Mallory and I work over in the north wings. I found a print-out in the computer room and wondered if it was yours?'

She held it out. Jock slowly pushed his chair back.

'Oh, uh, okay,' he said, taking the paper.

The badge at the centre front of his hat was from the Stockman's Hall of Fame. Mallory tried not to stare at the others, or to try to count how many there were.

'Thank you,' he said quickly, folding the paper in half.

Mallory smiled. 'You know Ernest Flint?'

'He's just down the hall, but he doesn't know how to work the computer.' Jock paused. 'I think he's allergic.'

Mallory laughed. 'I'm just glad to see someone's using the computer room. We tried to organise a course last year but there was some funding problem. And I always thought it shouldn't be locked, but they're concerned about theft or something.'

Jock's expression warmed. 'Sounds like standard bureaucracy. Though maybe it's my collection has them worried?'

He gestured at a set of movie cases on the shelf, where *Ocean's Eleven*, *The Italian Job*, *The Thomas Crown Affair*, *The Bank Job* and *3000 Miles to Graceland* poked out their spines.

'Wow,' Mallory said, with a laugh. 'I'm seeing a trend there. Like a good heist?'

'Don't worry. Not planning anything.'

Mallory winked. 'I won't tell anyone. Don't you have a great view up here,' she said, catching a glimpse through the glass. He had one of the north-east windows that faced the ocean, a bright expanse of cobalt blue framed in gum trees. Below, the gardeners were still working on the fallen branches.

'It's not bad, is it?' he said. 'The storms are spectacular. And I can see the sun come up over the water.' He blew out an audible breath. To Mallory, he seemed a little reserved, and was more comfortable now she wasn't facing him.

'You ever paint it?' she asked, nodding towards the paints on the bookcase, and choosing not to think about storms.

'Oh, no, just the models,' he said. 'You know, I've seen you around downstairs, when the kids visit.'

'Have you? I'm sorry if I haven't said hello. I'm always running around making sure no one is missing, and no stray guinea pigs, that sort of thing. I'll try to do better today.' She gave him an encouraging smile.

'Right you are, then.'

Mallory looked around. 'This room is really nice. How did you get the changes past the board?'

Jock gave her a sly smile. 'You know the phrase "better to ask forgiveness than permission"?'

'I see,' Mallory said, nodding and laughing. She admired a touch of subversion. 'You know, these models are very good. Would you ever be interested in teaching a class—' She broke off, and took a breath, remembering that she wasn't going to be the Engagement Manager. 'Well, anyway, my son's very interested in models, though mostly trains. He comes in sometimes when the babysitter drops him off here at the end of my shift. Would it be all right if we came by sometime? Maybe you could give him a few pointers.'

Jock smiled. 'Anytime.'

By the time Mallory left Jock's room, she'd completely forgotten about that piece of paper.

Chapter 2

MALLORY ARRIVED TWENTY MINUTES EARLY TO THE airport, jangling with excitement. She smoothed her hair in the Corolla's rear-view mirror. Was the dress too much? Too late now if it was. She had to force her wobbly knees to carry her all the way to the terminal, changing the welcome poster between hands so that her clammy fingers wouldn't warp the cardboard.

She camped out by the arrivals rail, imagining Harry flying through the door. She would catch him up in an endless hug and press the softness of his hair against her cheek. In her mind, she went over and over what she would say to Duncan, the apologies she'd offer for any part she'd played in him leaving. Two weeks before, Duncan's timetable had been so tight, they'd not even had time for a coffee in the airport café.

'I'm sorry, I can't, Mal,' he'd said then, and he really had looked sorry, and tired too, in his beaten jeans and polo shirt at the end of a seventeen-hour journey. No one would have known he was the CEO of a hot software company he'd built from scratch. 'But we need to talk about everything. Can we do that in two weeks?' He'd given her an uncertain smile, the same one he always used when he wasn't sure of his reception. She'd agreed, nearly breathless with possibilities. She'd known then that he wanted them to try again.

So Mallory was ready to talk, to be calm and mature, and not to repeat the questions of the past year that had so often prompted only silence. Impatiently, she watched a previous flight's passengers dribbling out of customs, searching for their loved ones in the crowd. A few people strode towards the taxi rank alone, and Mallory could only feel sad for them.

Time dragged on, and the crowd thinned. Mallory paced, down to the end of the terminal and back. Oh, why did she have to be early? Waiting was just awful. Finally, the board said the flight had landed. She tried to do the maths in her head. How long would customs take? Half an hour at most, perhaps?

The first passengers appeared after twenty-five minutes. Mallory pushed her way back to the rail, bouncing on her feet with the 'Welcome Back Harry and Duncan' sign ready. She measured each shadow through the frosted glass wall, hope surging with every adult–child pair. After an hour, when she was the only one still waiting, Mallory dropped the sign. Three texts to Duncan had gone unanswered. Had she made some mistake?

She checked the flight number again. The airline. Maybe they were simply stuck in customs. Oh no, had Harry brought in something he shouldn't have? Or worse, had they missed the flight? Mallory groaned at the idea. She couldn't bear having to go home alone again and come back later. But surely Duncan would have let her know? They must just be delayed in customs.

The woman behind the airline's enquiry counter was sympathetic but firm. 'I'm sorry, I can't give out any inform-ation about passengers. Privacy, you understand.'

'But it's my son, and he's only five. I wanted to know if they were still waiting for bags or something.'

The woman's expression momentarily softened. 'He's travelling alone?'

'No . . . with my husband. I'm supposed to pick them both up.'

The woman shook her head. All that she could confirm was that, yes, the plane had landed, and it was the same one as the flight information Mallory had.

Mallory backed away, dejected. How much longer should she wait? The airline counter had told her that passengers couldn't take calls in customs, but she called Duncan's mobile anyway. It went straight to voicemail. Of course. Slightly encouraged, she waited through another half-hour. But when a new flight was disgorging its passengers, desperation set in. She tried his mobile four more times, then scrolled through her phone for the New York number. Duncan had a housekeeper called Maria; maybe she could confirm whether they had made the flight.

The line only rang once before it picked up. 'Hello?' said a male voice. Mallory's relief morphed to confusion. 'Who is this?' the man insisted, his voice thick with sleep. 'Hello?'

She took a quick breath. 'It's Mallory,' she managed. 'Duncan, it's Mal.'

In the long pause that followed, Mallory heard sheets rustling. She imagined him sitting up in bed and rubbing his eyes. 'Mal. It's four in the morning,' he said.

'Did you miss the flight? I'm at the airport.'

'Ah, shit,' he said, as though he'd just forgotten an appointment at the dentist. 'I meant to call you. But then we had this meeting with the VC guys and things were intense for a few days. I forgot.'

'You forgot?' Bright streaks of annoyance and hurt and relief shot through Mallory's heart, forming a muddy indecipherable emotion. 'Duncan, I was so worried! I didn't know where you were.'

'We're right here.' He had a tone now, as though she was being melodramatic. 'But I did mean to call you. Harry's staying here, Mal.'

'What?' Mallory tried to grasp what he was saying. 'Does he want to stay longer?'

The other end of the line muffled, but she could still hear Duncan's footsteps, the sound of a door catch opening and closing. Then the creaking of a leather chair. He must have closed himself in his office.

He let out a sigh. 'Please believe that I didn't want to do this on the phone, but I don't think I can possibly get away for a while. I think it's better for everyone if we keep things as they are right now. Harry's happy. And you'll have an easier time, too.'

'What are you talking about?' she asked. 'Harry's got school on Monday.'

'You're not listening, Mal,' he said, very calm, very reasonable. 'I'm saying he has a school here. We already talked about this possibility.'

Mallory felt her eyebrows crush together. 'When did we talk about it?'

'At the café, at the airport, two weeks ago. When I asked about Harry living in New York. You said you'd be open to it.'

'I never said that . . .' she began, but suddenly she really couldn't remember what she'd said two weeks ago. She'd been so busy thinking about the possibilities with Duncan, of the three of them being a family again, she hadn't even finished her coffee. Had she given him the idea that he could do this? Had she misinterpreted his words as a romantic gesture, thinking he meant the two of them should try again, when really he meant something else?

'I never meant that he would just stay there now,' she said, through a wave of nauseating panic. 'He's supposed to come home.'

'That's not what you said, Mal,' he said, with an exasperated sigh. 'Look, I understand this isn't the best way of doing things. But I really do have it all sorted out. Harry loves it here. He can go to an amazing school just a few blocks from the office. He's already made some friends this last fortnight. He can have a home here that he can only dream about in Australia. Opportunities. We talked about this. He won't have to grow up in such a tiny place, and it will be easier for you too. Of course, I want you to be free to call anytime, visit anytime you like. But him staying here is best for everyone.'

Mallory's back met the glass wall of the terminal with a thud. She pressed a shaking hand to her forehead. What was he talking about? He was the one who'd left her and Harry for his company's big chance in New York. He was the one who'd said their lives had moved apart. She couldn't fathom what he was doing.

'Let me talk to Harry,' she said in a rush. 'Please.'

'He's asleep, Mal.'

She had the awful sense of finality, that Duncan was about to close the shutter on this conversation without any resolution. 'He gets up early. Please. He'll be awake. I just need to hear his voice.'

'He's only just adjusted to the time zone,' Duncan said, firm. 'Now, as I said, you feel free to call anytime you like. He loves seeing you on Skype. We'll need to iron out the small details. We will. But that will have to be later. I've got an early meeting. Take care, Mal.'

With that, the line clicked. Mallory re-dialled, again and again, and heard the engaged signal.

She lowered her phone in cold, stomach-sinking disbelief. A few people milled past with trolleys and bags, oblivious to Mallory's ridiculous dreams now lying like shredded paper at her feet. It had all been a fantasy, just like the faint lingering scent of Harry's shampoo she could almost smell in the air.

Chapter 3

THE NEXT MORNING MALLORY SAT CHEWING HER NAILS IN the offices of Turner & Bodie, a family law firm in the outer suburbs. The air-conditioning was turned off for the weekend, and the atmosphere was thick and still. She was convinced all of this was some mistake . . . but she was also desperate for information. Bridget had made the appointment after Mallory had called her from the airport. Bridget knew someone, who knew someone who was the brother of one of the partners, so another someone had come in specially on a Saturday to see Mallory.

The slim young lawyer across the desk wore a dark suit and a pair of thick-rimmed glasses. While her attire was disturbingly similar to Mrs Crawley's, she managed to exude a calm confidence as she listened to Mallory's story, making notes on her yellow pad. The framed certificates on the wall oozed authority, so by the time Mallory finished speaking, she felt reassured that all the confusion would be over soon.

'Let me recap,' the lawyer said, flicking over her pages. 'After Mr Cook moved out last year, the arrangement has always been that Harry lived with you?'

'Yes. He moved to New York and Harry stayed with me. Duncan said he didn't have the resources for us over there.'

'Has he ever paid maintenance?'

Mallory shook her head. 'He didn't have any income while he was building his business. I was the one working.'

'What about after he moved out? When the business took off?'

'Um, well, he said that they had a lot of start-up costs, and he wasn't drawing a salary yet. And he always looked after Harry while I worked before that, so I think I would have been the one paying him.'

She expected to see judgement, the kind Bridget always served up when Mallory talked about Duncan and his business, which Mallory had bankrolled since she was eighteen. Even after Harry came along, she'd worked nights and weekends to keep Duncan's hopes alive. She had only enjoyed momentary vindication when his start-up attracted a game-changing investment, before he'd moved out. She had walked around like a zombie, devastated and embarrassed, but as the weeks went by, she could see the stress he'd been under with the company, that he needed space for a while. Bridget thought those concessions were madness.

'What sort of man happily lets a new mother go out to work while he sits at home earning nothing?' Bridget had said more than once. Mallory could only shrug.

Now, the lawyer seemed unsurprised as she scratched down notes. She pushed up her glasses. 'From what you've told me, the facts seem straightforward. You've always had full custody by mutual agreement after you separated. Your son went to visit Mr Cook with the understanding he would return yesterday, and now Mr Cook has declared he's taking custody without your agreement. Fortunately, the States is a signatory to the Hague Convention, so we can lodge recovery orders and have them recognised by an American court. We should also apply to have Harry on the Family Law Watchlist, in case they do happen to return to Australia. After that,' she said, 'I'd want to consult one of the senior partners about contacting the Attorney-General's Department to put in place some more long-term measures.'

The complicated terms hung over Mallory like storm clouds, and she hated the word 'separated'. She didn't want to have to do any of this, couldn't imagine how Harry would feel to be dragged through court proceedings. Surely Duncan would realise what a mistake he'd made before it came to that?

'This isn't like him,' she said, hoping desperately she was right. 'Duncan wouldn't take Harry away. I'm sure he's just misunderstood something I said.'

'It's very common to feel that way,' the lawyer said carefully. 'And it is possible, but I don't want you to be surprised if you find that your husband knows exactly what he's doing, and if he's quite refractory to reason. Sometimes people do incredibly cruel and inexplicable things when marriages break up, and it comes as a complete surprise.'

Mallory swallowed, her body rejecting the idea like a bad oyster. 'Okay.'

The lawyer took off her glasses and rubbed the bridge of her nose. 'Mallory, I do want you to be prepared. While the process is clear – we can lodge the documents in a week, and organise a barrister overseas – it's also expensive. Very expensive. And if he decides to challenge, it could become very long and involved.'

Mallory opened her mouth to say Duncan wouldn't have the money, but closed it again. She really didn't know what he had.

'How much?' she asked.

The lawyer named a figure that was most of what Mallory made in a year, then added, 'But if he challenges, more, and the whole process could take months. Are you ready for that?'

Mallory's laugh came out under the pressure of her nerves, before a noose of fear tightened around her throat. 'How could he possibly challenge it?' she whispered. 'I supported him for six years. I worked nights and weekends, even when Harry was a baby. I just can't believe that he'd do this. He always said when the business took off, he'd make it all up to me.'

An involuntary tear spilled down her face. Wordlessly, the lawyer pushed a tissue box across the desk.

'Mallory,' she said gently, 'people do the most hideous things when their families break down. Sadly, this isn't a special case. It's our job to help you.'

'Do you think he's right?' Mallory asked, suddenly full of doubt. 'That Harry would be better off there? That he wouldn't have to see how hard it is to make ends meet? He could afford better schools, all that stuff.'

'That's really not for me to say,' the lawyer said, but Mallory heard a note of disgust. 'Might be better if he'd chosen to send you some of his new riches, or to discuss it with you first. I don't know how he could challenge it, but he might. You are clearly not neglectful, but he could allege something harder to prove, like mental instability, which might mean you have to sit a psychiatric evaluation.

'And that's not all, I'm afraid,' the lawyer continued, her expression grim. 'Even when we recover Harry, you may need a parenting order to ensure he stays here with you. In that case, it could be five times as much.'

It was almost the price of a house. Mallory had no more words. She beat a hasty retreat, saying she would think about it.

•

Mallory spent the journey back to the cottage wondering where she could find that impossible kind of money. All avenues seemed to converge on winning the lotto. When her thoughts took a dark turn towards casinos, she pulled over and walked around on the footpath to get a grip.

She arrived home feeling as though she'd just worked a twelve-hour overnight shift. Autumn was sliding towards winter and a chill blanketed the cottage under the trees, colouring the world bleak. The iron roof was dull, the windows dark, and the shaggy coat of climbing jasmine too heavy for the leaning timbers to hold up. Mallory had the involuntary thought to search for Harry's warmer pyjamas, which led to further tears.

Inside, the rooms were cold and empty, the bare boards creaking. The kitchen bulb blew when she flicked on the switch. She gathered Harry's old bear to her chest, just to have something of him to hold. His toys were all from op shops; every spare cent had gone on babysitters this past year. Now that he'd started school, she had been saving slowly, but she didn't have anything close to the amount the lawyer was talking about, and there wasn't anything to sell. All the furniture was second hand. She and Duncan had been married in a quick civil ceremony, and they'd never got around to a ring. All their friends had been just out of school, so there hadn't been any expensive gifts. Her car was barely worth scrap, and she needed a vehicle for the relief shifts she did at the respite centre. After her mother's habits, she had been too afraid to apply for credit cards. She had only two accounts: one for expenses, the other for savings. Expenses had just enough for groceries before her next pay. In savings, she had the bare germination of a one-day home deposit. It wasn't enough.

Time evaporated in her bewilderment. When she came back to reality, she was out in the yard with an old serving spoon she used as a trowel in her hand, weeds from the vegetable patch in an uprooted pile. The sun was going down, the chickens were happily scratching around for worms, and her fingernails were clogged with dirt. She sighed and returned inside to clean up and face the problem. She had to find a way.

Twenty minutes later, when she was examining online interest rates on personal loans and feeling sick to her toenails, Bridget knocked on the door, bearing a cardboard box of fruit and vegetables.

'Unwanted proceeds of the co-op haul. I thought you could use it,' she said, depositing the box on the kitchen bench and automatically filling the kettle. 'Now, what did the lawyer say?'

Mallory relayed the information numbly, as if she were out of her own body, while Bridget made tea and pushed a mug in front of her. When Mallory finished, Bridget sat back, apparently too shocked to make her customary jab at Duncan.

'Do you think he'll fight it?' she said.

Mallory rubbed her finger over a crack in the countertop. 'I don't know.'

'I was going to say I'd lend you the money,' Bridget said, 'but I never imagined it could be that much.'

Mallory could only shake her head. Regardless of where the money came from, she could be paying it back forever. 'I know you'll think I'm crazy, but I know that if Duncan and I were just able to be in the same place, none of this would be happening. He isn't like this, Bridge. New York's just so far away. It's never the same on the phone or Skype.'

'Well, I'm not sure about that. But I wouldn't blame you if you just got on a plane,' Bridget said. 'What can he do if you just show up?'

Bridget left after an hour, but the idea wouldn't. Mallory paced the house. She'd thought about going to New York before, but not exactly like this. It was supposed to be them all going, together. Mallory had never been overseas. The prospect of going on her own was daunting, and a flight to the States was expensive. Then again, it wasn't as expensive as the legal fees, and if she and Duncan could just talk face to face . . .

She pulled herself up. She couldn't just leave on no notice. What about work? And besides, she should really try to talk to Duncan again. This could still all be a misunderstanding.

She waited for the clock to drag around to nine-thirty, when she opened Skype with a shaking hand and dialled, half expecting no one would pick up.

'Mummy! I heard the beeps.'

Harry!

His voice shot sunshine beams of joy through her heart. The picture took a few seconds to resolve, long enough for Mallory to swipe away her tears. Harry was kneeling on a black leather chair, the one in Duncan's study in front of the computer. 'Hi, baby!' she said. 'How are you?'

For a few minutes, Harry talked about all the things he had been doing – eating hot dogs, going to Central Park and Coney Island and the aquarium, some of the time with Maria because Daddy had been working, but he'd seen Daddy's new office, too, and been allowed to play with the photocopier. He was wearing a shirt with 'I love New York' on the front, the *love* replaced with a red heart. It tore at Mallory: Harry clearly understood nothing about what was going on.

'Daddy says I can stay, so when are you coming, Mummy?' Harry said finally.

'I'm not sure, baby,' she said, choking up. To see his little trusting face through the monitor was too much. 'Can I talk to Daddy?'

'Sure, Mum!' Harry climbed down off the desk chair, and she heard him call for Duncan. The chair slowly swung around, revealing an abstract print on the wall behind. Beneath it was a graceful glass vase atop a wooden cabinet with brass handles. The whole thing looked expensive, and would probably be awarded tens on a renovation reality show.

She eventually heard Duncan, somewhere off-camera, saying, 'What have I said about coming into my office?' Harry's response wasn't audible, but Mallory tensed.

Harry's face popped back into view, looking contrite. 'Dad says I have to get ready now. Bye, Mum, I miss you!'

'I miss you too, baby—'

But he was gone. After a long pause, when Mallory's heart was beating so hard her chest ached, Duncan appeared, a larger, harder version of that same face. He didn't sit down, just leaned on the desk. All she could see was the powder blue of his shirt, a striped pink tie hanging down. A thick watchband she didn't recognise circled his wrist.

He ducked his head into view, straightening his tie as he looked into the screen. 'This'll have to be quick, Mal. We're on our way out.' A little frown of concentration gathered between his brows. His gaze ran off to the left as he clicked the mouse. 'Just closing a few windows. I'm running late.'

A dagger stabbed through Mallory's heart. She took a huge breath, trying not to be rushed. 'This early?' she said, sounding upbeat. 'Must be the big bucks.' Duncan had once joked he wouldn't get out of his pyjamas before nine unless he was being paid the big bucks.

'It's after seven-thirty,' he said, distracted, missing the old joke. 'I've got a meeting at nine downtown, and Harry has a new music class to get to first.' He leaned away from the monitor. 'Harry!' he called. 'Brush your teeth please, sport! Maria's waiting.'

'Duncan, we need to talk. Right now, please.'

Duncan paused, and looked back into the screen.

'I didn't agree to this,' Mallory said. 'I don't know what sort of misunderstanding we had, but Harry can't stay with you. He lives with me, and his school is here. That's been our agreement since you left. You can't just up and change it. He needs to come home.'

'We agreed that—'

'No, we didn't! You didn't ask me about any of this, and I certainly didn't agree to Harry staying there for anything more than the two-week visit. Now, I want to know when he's flying back. As soon as possible.'

A pause. 'Are you finished there?' Duncan's voice was so cold, Mallory shrank. She'd only heard that low, angry voice from him once before, and it brought the memory flooding back. They'd been at a dinner with some potential investors in his company years ago. The night had been a big deal for Duncan, the first serious sign anyone might be prepared to invest in the business. Mallory had known that, but she'd also been so tired that night, shy and wrong-footed at the fancy party, uncomfortable in a borrowed dress. She hadn't known what to say to people and probably wasn't in her right mind, after two bad nights with Harry, a double shift and the stress of leaving him with a sitter. In her nerves, she'd told some stories from her work, and somewhere between Mrs Connelly's enema and Mr King's sailor-swearing, and the polite avoidant eyes of the dinner guests, she realised this probably wasn't appropriate conversation. Duncan's mouth had been very tight as he'd drawn her aside. 'That's enough, Mal,' he'd said. 'For God's sake, I'm asking these people for money. And one of them's the Liberal Party president. Have a bit of thought.'

She'd been so ashamed of embarrassing him then.

Now, trying not to quail, she said, 'He's my son, Duncan.'

'And he's mine, too,' Duncan countered. 'I'm giving him a better life here. You have a good hard think about it, Mal, and you know I'm right. We talked about this. You can't just change your mind either.'

'No, it isn't better! And we haven't!' Mallory said, finally suspecting that there hadn't been any miscommunication at all, that maybe the lawyer was right. 'You can't just take him, can't uproot him from his life here.'

'Settle down,' Duncan said. 'And don't take that combative tone with me, Mal. How do you think Harry will feel to hear you? You're confusing him.'

She frowned. 'How the hell am I confusing him?'

'He needs to settle in here. If he's hanging out for calls all the time, and if you're telling him he should come home, it's mixed messages. You'll just upset him.'

'I'm upsetting my own child by talking to him?'

'Well, yes.'

'I'm his mother, Duncan. He lives with me. He's lived with me his whole life. You took off a year ago. Why are you being such a heartless bastard? Just let him come home!'

Duncan heaved a sigh, as if he was the most put-upon man in the world. 'If you can't acknowledge your part in this, I want you to stop calling.'

'What?'

'At least for a while. You're not helping anyone.'

A bruising fist thumped into Mallory's stomach. 'You can't cut me off and be so unreasonable. I'm speaking to a lawyer.'

Duncan didn't even flinch. 'Mal, I'm *being* reasonable. You're the one being dramatic. Think about it. Really, think. Harry is better off here. And if you try and argue differently, and get lawyers involved, then I'll have to raise my concerns about your fitness.'

Mallory's mouth opened, stunned.

'That's not fair—' she began.

'We have to go. I won't have him singled out because he's the kid late to class. And don't call again.'

The video feed vanished, replaced by the profile photo of Duncan with Harry, incongruously smiling. Desperately,

Mallory hit 'call' again. It rang and rang, and rang out. She tried again, and this time the call dropped immediately. Duncan was now offline.

For a long minute, Mallory couldn't move. Of all the outcomes, this wasn't the one she'd expected. Beyond him cutting her off, she glimpsed that he'd been calculating in doing this. Deliberate.

She sat back in her chair, listening to the kitchen clock *tick, tick, tick,* around five whole minutes. And then, without thinking, she opened her browser and clicked through to an airline booking site. A week ago, when she'd been off in the hopeful dreamland that Duncan might ask her to come to New York, she'd applied for a visa waiver, so there was nothing to stop her. *Click, click* on book and pay.

Bridget had said she would get on a plane. And that was exactly what Mallory was going to do.

Chapter 4

MALLORY MANAGED TO DOZE ON THE FIRST HALF OF THE flight, but the closer she came to Los Angeles, the more sleep eluded her. When the flight attendant was clearing trays from the dinner meal, and other passengers were nodding off under grey blankets, she was thinking through her plan for the fifth time. She had to change planes in Los Angeles, then once she arrived in New York she would take the subway to Duncan's apartment. Or maybe she would have enough cash for a taxi. That might be faster than working out the subway. It wasn't much of a plan, so she spent the rest of her time obsessing over Duncan, and what on earth had happened.

After he'd left a year ago, Mallory had never once gone looking for information about him online; nothing could be worse than reading about his success. Once or twice, she'd idly typed his name into Google and waited just long enough to see the results come back before she closed the window, her heart pulsing with the hurt of his leaving.

But after that last Skype call, she couldn't help herself. She had clearly missed something. When she and Duncan had first met, he'd been an aspiring entrepreneur, a generous, funny man who made her feel like the whole world was made of stars. Something had clearly changed. She had to understand what. She filled the time to her flight finding and saving articles.

His LinkedIn profile hadn't given her much she didn't already know: CEO of Iron Gate Software. His Twitter account was mostly reposts of business-related news articles. Finding anything else was surprisingly hard.

Mallory waded past search results for a few academics and lawyers with the same name. When she eventually found an article mentioning *her* Duncan Cook, it made her eyes cross, full of dry business jargon about market potential and stock options and promising start-ups. Iron Gate was only one of the 'one to watch' companies in the article, but the writer took the time to mention Duncan's energy and all-out commitment to success, yet his down-to-earth casual approach to the workplace. That was still the Duncan she had known: working slavish hours, but opposed to the formal stuffiness of traditional business. Now, reading the article for the fourth time revealed nothing new. She sighed and leaned back in her seat. Outside the window, the world was starless, only the flash of the plane's lights breaking the night.

Far across that darkness, phones were ringing in the Federal Aviation Administration offices all over the USA. As Mallory flew over the International Date Line, an ominous bulge appeared on the side of a volcanic cone near Lassen Peak in the Redding area of California. It was the same mountain that had appeared on the newsfeed Mallory had watched in the Silky Oaks lounge; the US Geological Survey had been concerned about increased seismic activity in the region for weeks. Then, at 5:08 am local time, a lateral blast erupted from the volcano, creating a debris avalanche and a cloud of fine silica and ash fourteen miles high, which began drifting across the USA at the speed of a late-model passenger car.

By the time Mallory next woke to a pink and apricot sunrise on the wing, airspace was being shut down all across the west coast. Emergency services were scrambling to keep daredevil sightseers away from the mountain. The captain made the first announcement: something about a volcano, but they were being allowed to land. Mallory raked her fingers through her hair as the cabin crew served juice as if nothing was happening. Crisis seemingly averted.

But when she spilled out into the LAX terminal, chaos appeared to have set up shop and sold tickets. Customs was backlogged with a great sea of people in subdued silence. After an endless wait in the barely moving line, she finally stumbled through the exit chute, and found more milling crowds. The air smelled of heat and sweat. All thoughts of Harry and Duncan momentarily evaporated.

She rushed down the concourse until she found a set of arrival and departure monitors, the screens awash with red-and-yellow 'Cancelled' messages flashing down the rows. Like so many other stranded travellers, she scanned, hoping against all hope that her connection would be the exception. But, no. Cancelled.

Pushing through the crowds took forever and a stress-flush burned up her neck and cheeks. Great ribbons of people and bags streamed from every airline desk. Complications were accumulating like bricks, building a wall in the way of New York. This couldn't be happening. Seriously? A volcano?

As someone who'd just left the desk walked back along the line, Mallory put out a desperate arm. 'Excuse me, what did they tell you?'

'Everything's on hold,' said the man, with a philosophical shrug. 'The ash cloud is drifting right across the country. There goes my trip to Atlanta!'

When Mallory finally reached the desk, the frazzled clerk could only confirm all the flights to New York had been cancelled and they were organising luggage return. They could offer a flight back to Australia, which she would have to pay for, or she could stay and wait. Mallory asked when the flights would be back, ready to accept a day, maybe two.

The clerk just laughed. 'Ask the volcano!' he said. 'Next!'

Mallory closed her eyes. She was on the wrong side of a foreign country with only a few hundred dollars to her name. For the first time since Harry had left to visit Duncan, she felt truly and utterly alone.

She willed herself to calm down. There must be other options. All the car-hire desks had posted hastily printed signs saying they were completely out of stock, so she connected the free wi-fi on her phone and looked up trains to New York. She bit her lip when she saw the information: it would take nearly three days and cost three hundred dollars. Even so, it had to be better than hanging around in an airport. She would run out of money paying airport food prices in less time.

By the time she'd selected the fare, the site told her that seat had been sold. The next-best deal was a hundred dollars more. She swore under her breath and accepted, plugged in her debit card details, and hit purchase. The screen paused for a long time. Mallory watched, knowing she should not press back or interrupt or even breathe wrong while the electronic brain processed her details.

Then it declined. Mallory said a very bad word.

Muttering, she checked her account balance: enough to cover the ticket. She tried and failed to book three more times. Exasperated, she changed the last cash in her wallet to US dollars and called the train booking service. When the card declined there too, she finally used a handful of dollars to call the bank in Australia from a payphone, nervous about her mobile's credit.

'Ah, well, there's the problem,' said the operator with unnecessary enthusiasm. 'The account has been frozen.'

'Frozen?' said Mallory. 'But how could it be frozen?'

The operator cleared her throat. 'Well ... sometimes it can be a creditor with a court order—'

'I don't have any creditors.'

'Let me just look in the notes. Oh, I see. Requested by Mr Duncan Cook, the joint account holder.'

Mallory pressed a hand to her head. This wasn't happening. Her skin burned hot against her palm. This wasn't happening. 'Why would he do that?'

'Well, most likely the request was made pending a dispute with the joint account holder.'

'Meaning me?'

'Well, yes. It's just a temporary freeze. It will automatically be removed after thirty days if there's no further action.'

'I'm stranded in LA,' she said, a quiver in her voice. 'I'm sitting in the terminal. My flight's been cancelled and I just want to book a train and I can't because my husband froze my last four hundred dollars?'

'I'm sorry to hear that,' the operator continued professionally after a short pause. 'This must be very frustrating. The volcano seems to be making a mess. I just saw it on the news.'

No matter what Mallory said, or how she pleaded, nothing could be done. She ended the call with her whole body hollowed out to the husk. Duncan taking Harry had stolen her heart, and now this had scraped out the last of her dignity.

Angrily, she dialled Duncan again and again on Skype. No answer. She googled the number for his company in New York, but the receptionist only got through telling her he was out of the office before her money ran out. Mallory closed her eyes against the tears. She was willing to bet that he would never answer her there anyway.

In that moment, standing in a cloud of desperation by the out-of-credit payphone, she remembered a resident they'd had at Silky Oaks a few years ago: Glenda, an American woman with early onset Parkinson's disease. Mallory had taken to chatting to her on the night shifts, and they played cards together, which Glenda insisted was good for her motor skills. Glenda would sometimes tell stories about her life in America, jovial nothings about the wonders of soul food or the coast in her native Washington state, nothing too personal. Then, one night, Mallory had asked how she'd come to Australia. Glenda had gone very quiet, then told her a long black comedy of dominoes: her husband had been diagnosed with cancer; Glenda had lost her job because there was no one else to take care of him. Then, she'd been evicted because she had no job, and nowhere else would give her a lease. The two of them had ended up in a shelter in the middle of a bitter winter, her husband growing sicker and sicker. Eventually, they'd been able to contact a relative and make the journey to Australia, where they'd stayed.

Mallory remembered the faraway look in Glenda's eyes as she said, 'You never know what's going to happen, Mallory. You think everything is fine one day, and then life knocks your knees right out, and you're tumbling down and down, and there ain't a damn thing you can do about it.'

Mallory knew now what she'd meant. Three days ago, her life had been manageable and stable, on track for a promotion and a family reunion. She'd never been aware of how fragile it had all been, and now the card house had collapsed. If she'd just had a credit card . . . but even the thought of credit made her break out in hives. She heard ringing phones and saw the shadows of big men coming to knock on her mother's door. It had never been an option.

With her account frozen, she couldn't even contemplate calling work to ask for an advance. Not to mention that it was the middle of the night in Brisbane. When she swallowed her embarrassment and thought to try Bridget, all the train tickets for the next week were sold out.

Only two choices remained. Fly home, or stay and hope.

•

Mallory sat on the toilet lid, her head slumped to the wall, listening to the repetitive *whoosh* of taps and hand dryers. She couldn't go back to Australia without Harry. She would have to camp here with all the other unfortunates until flights resumed. Just her and the two changes of clothes she had in her duffel bag, currently hanging on the back of the door.

But what if flights were weeks away? What would she eat? Where would she sleep? Mallory squeezed her eyes shut. She was so stupid. She'd been in such a hurry, she hadn't even thought to buy travel insurance.

She tore a square of toilet paper to blot her eyes. Her mission had been struck down by an act of God. Mallory wasn't particularly religious, but she worked with elderly people whose families had often forsaken them. She listened to their stories and wiped their unmentionables. What God would keep a mother – any mother, let alone a carer for the aged – from her child?

Mallory started as someone rattled the cubicle door, probably making sure she wasn't forgetting the waiting line. She swiped her eyes with the rough scrunched paper, sniffed, flushed, swung her bag over her shoulder, and opened the door. A few tired eyes in the queue flicked over her, pretending not to notice her puffy face. She squeezed past to a spare basin between a woman examining her lipstick, and an elderly lady wearing a cardigan in royal purple.

Mallory soaped her hands, thinking over the cash in her pocket. When she turned to the hand dryer, the old woman hadn't moved. She was staring into space, her brilliant white hair finger-waved in the front like a twenties flapper's, giving her face a distinguished frame. She looked fun, Mallory thought, with her bright cardigan and a long red skirt, but tired and lost. One hand clasped some papers to her chest.

Mallory touched her shoulder. 'Excuse me. Are you okay there?'

The woman shifted, her gaze unfocused. She slowly tracked across and finally met Mallory's gaze. After a second, she brightened.

'Mabel!' she said.

Mallory had worked with elders long enough to recognise someone in need of help. She pressed a hand to her chest. 'I'm Mallory. Are you waiting for someone?'

The woman brushed her forehead, as if trying to remember.

'Can you tell me your name?' Mallory asked.

No answer to that, either. Mallory appealed to the waiting line, but everyone shook their heads. The woman clutched Mallory's arm to steady herself, and Mallory patted the hand.

'Don't worry, we'll work it out. May I?' she asked, pointing to the papers. The woman slackened her grip and offered across what turned out to be a small stack of photos. They were old, some faded to sepia, others with folded corners and brown stains. Mallory flipped through pictures of dogs and cats, a goat, and two horses standing by a white fence rail.

'That's Agatha and Christie,' the woman said suddenly, pointing a trembling finger at the horses, her words carrying a trace of a southern accent. 'I have to feed them before dark. They get so riled up, waiting.'

'They're beautiful,' Mallory said. The next was a black-and-white wedding photo, the young couple standing under the spreading branches of a tree. The man wore a suit with a carnation pinned on his lapel, and a shy smile. The woman wore a grin, cat-eye glasses and a smooth white satin dress, her left hand holding a bouquet away, as if she were about to bowl an underarm pitch. On the back, *Zadie and Ernest, Sydney 1968* was written in faded fountain pen letters.

'Is this you?' Mallory asked, searching for a resemblance between the woman before her and the much younger face in the photograph. 'Zadie?'

'The flowers made me sneeze,' the woman said with a tremulous laugh, touching the small bouquet in the photo. 'I had to hold them down like that. I told Ernie that I was fine with it being just us, but he doesn't really understand. He's so set in his ideas.'

Zadie gave Mallory a beaming smile, as if all this made perfect sense. Mallory couldn't help smiling back.

'How about we see if we can find someone to make an announcement? There's plenty of time before dark, and you can tell me more about Agatha and Christie if you like.'

Mallory led Zadie slowly towards the doors, sure that someone would be searching for her already.

The terminal was more congested than ever. Zadie tightened her hand as Mallory paused to look for an airline help desk, and several people jostled past, shifting their shoulders to fit. Mallory reconsidered her plan, worried about them being knocked over, but she couldn't leave Zadie on her own. She was about to collar one of the passers-by when a man in a green fishing hat caught her eye. He was turned away, but clearly searching, back and forth, scanning between groups of people. His hat was covered in badges and with a frayed patch on the back brim, it looked just like the one Jock had been wearing at Silky Oaks . . .

He turned, and they locked eyes with a mutual jolt. It *was* Jock. Wrung out with all the drama, Mallory waved, glad to see any familiar face. And after a pause, with Jock squinting at her across the crowd, he raised a hand.

'Well,' he said, after pushing his way through, 'fancy meeting again like this.'

At the same moment, a booming call came from the left. 'Zadie? Zadie! There you are, thank God!'

The voice's imposing owner limped into view. Mallory's first impression was of a storybook giant: a tall, bad-tempered, grey-haired man with large ears, clearing the crowd with swings of his cane. But he was too neat for a giant – his hair was precisely combed, his checked shirt tucked in to grey dress pants and restrained with a polished brown belt. And despite his stature, he was frail. Mallory could see how one leg dragged, the thinness of the limb through the trouser leg, the heavy lean on the cane.

This man pulled to a stop, looming over Mallory, Zadie and Jock, the four of them creating an island in the slow tide of stranded passengers.

Zadie kept hold of Mallory's arm. 'I found Mabel,' she said.

The giant frowned and, after transferring his cane into the crook of his elbow, reached for Zadie's arm. 'Come on now, Zade. You can't just wander off like that.'

'She was in the ladies' bathroom, looking a bit lost. I'm Mallory,' Mallory added, observing the same heavy brow as the man in Zadie's photo. 'You must be Ernest? I just saw your wedding photo.'

The man with the cane looked at Mallory with a turned-down mouth, as if she'd just told him she'd been snooping around in his bedroom. Finally, he said, 'It's Ernie. Ernie Flint. Much obliged to you, young lady. Now, come along, Zadie.'

'Oh!' Mallory exclaimed. '*You're* Ernest Flint. From the itinerary.' She smiled encouragingly at Jock. In the middle of her own despair, this unexpected connection to Silky Oaks was a great comfort. But her declaration only produced a tense stare from Ernie.

'She's the one who found the print-out,' Jock said quickly. 'She works at Silky Oaks. How do you like those odds?'

Ernie's mouth dropped open in alarm. 'She does? What's she doing here?'

'Relax,' Jock said. 'She's not here to take you back. Or are you?'

'Take you back?' Mallory asked, confused, until Jock gave her a just-go-with-it wink. 'I mean . . . no?'

'Excellent, you see, Ern?' Jock said. 'Now, where are you headed?'

Mallory sighed. 'Nowhere, it seems. I was supposed to be in New York. Are you stuck too?'

'That depends,' he said. 'Would you go back into the ladies' and see if someone called Fiona is in there?'

'Fiona?'

'Yes, please. Blue blouse, black trousers, blonde hair in a ponytail.'

So Mallory did. 'Nope,' she reported five minutes later. 'Two Fionas, but none matching that description.'

'Dammit,' Jock muttered. 'I was afraid of that.'

'Who's Fiona?'

But Jock and Ernie were engrossed in another conversation that involved no words, just eyebrow raises, small head shakes and fingers rubbing at temples.

Finally, Jock said, 'What do you think, Ern?'

Ernie gave a one-shouldered shrug. 'It's a foolhardy idea. But if you think she's the only option.'

With that, he led Zadie away. While Mallory was still perplexed by what was going on, she couldn't help but be touched by the way Ernie protected Zadie, even with their slow, limping steps. Zadie looked back over her shoulder and waved. Mallory waved back.

'What was all that about?' she asked Jock.

'Well, you said you're stuck here, right?'

'Yes.' Mallory raised her hands hopelessly. 'I couldn't get a car, or a train, so I guess I'm waiting it out. Maybe it'll only be a day or two. That's possible, right?'

Jock laughed. 'Don't you remember Eyjafjallajökull?'

'Remember what?'

'The Icelandic volcano that blew in twenty-ten. Could be weeks yet, and then there's the backlog of passengers to shift.'

Mallory's mouth opened and closed without a sound. 'Are you serious?' she said faintly. She'd be on starvation rations to last even a week in the airport with her cash reserves.

'What if I told you that we could all leave, right now? We have a car, we just need someone to drive, and to help out. Maybe we can solve each other's problems. How about it?'

'You need a driver?' Mallory frowned at him, waiting for the catch, and suddenly thinking about his heist DVD collection. 'You're not planning on robbing a bank, are you?'

Jock laughed. 'Partner in crime, if you want to think of it that way.'

As Mallory considered his offer, thinking about Harry, she realised that she probably *would* rob a bank at this point, if it meant she could get to New York.

'Let's talk,' she said.

•

'It's just a little road trip, plain and simple,' Jock explained when they were all seated at a café table.

Mallory's hopes dimmed. 'But I need to be in New York as soon as possible. I can't possibly do a leisurely road trip.'

Jock glanced at Ernie. 'We never intended to drive either. Ernie and Zadie are heading to Nashville, and I've my own rendezvous further down the road. So, I figure, you drive us all to Nashville, then you can hire your own car, or fly if they're running again. It'll only take a few days. We'll still get there long before all this flight business sorts itself.'

Mallory gulped her steaming cup of black coffee like it was water, trying to cut through the long-haul fog and work out if this really was an option. Finally, she shook her head. 'I haven't got any money for hiring a car,' she said. 'I'll just end up stranded in Nashville.'

Jock sat back. 'This is your department,' he said to Ernie.

Ernie turned his bushy scrutinising brows on Mallory. He hadn't said much to this point, but he hardly needed to: he had the brand of stare that belonged to school principals and High Court judges. 'I'll offer you a simple contract,' he said. 'You drive us to Nashville. Two thousand dollars is yours when we get there. We'll cover the hotels and meals on the way.'

Jock made to say something, but Ernie cut him off. 'That's the offer,' he said.

Mallory's mind raced with possibilities. 'How long did you say it will take?'

'Four days, I think, down the interstate,' Jock said, showing her a map on his smart phone. She squinted at the screen as he scrolled eastwards across the continental United States. She had no idea exactly how far it was, but she'd already made up her mind. The money was more than enough to fly from Nashville, or drive, or take a bus. She'd still have some cash when she reached New York, which she would no doubt need to fly Harry home. Driving also had advantages: no one could cancel the journey or dictate a timetable.

'All right,' she said. 'But I don't really know any of you from Silky Oaks. What care do you need from me?'

'Nothing really for me,' Jock put in quickly. 'Ernie—'

'Can answer for himself,' Ernie grumbled. 'Had a stroke. Right-side muscle weakness. Help with dressing, toileting, and two-handed activities.'

Mallory noted how he removed the pronouns, so it wouldn't have to feel like he was talking about himself – clearly a sensitive topic – but he was also clear and precise. He seemed to have a grip on everything, which was encouraging.

'Zadie,' he went on, 'has . . . early stages.'

Alzheimer's. Mallory nodded. 'Does she have any problems with balance?'

'Occasionally,' he said. 'Mostly it's memory problems, with good spells of clarity here and there. Tends to be worse in the evening. But her medication is working well at the moment.'

Except for wandering, Mallory thought. But Zadie couldn't wander if they were in a car, and if Jock could take care of himself it sounded very doable.

'And what if her medication—'

'I'm a doctor,' Ernie said, cutting her off. 'If medication needs adjusting, I can look at it.' He wore his scowl like a favourite outfit. 'Will that be all with the questions?'

Mallory downed the rest of the coffee. She looked at the three of them. She could say no and stay with the thousands of other stranded travellers. Or, she could take this chance. 'Let's go.'

And that was that. Even with their slow progress through the terminal, Mallory's mood lifted, her chest full of new hope and relief. All around, people were going nowhere, but not her. She was on her way. Crisis averted.

She carried this unsullied optimism right up until Jock fell into step beside her. 'Thank you,' he said. 'Now, tell me, have you driven on the right side of the road before?'

Chapter 5

Mallory never guessed leaving LA would be such an opera of wrong notes. She had grown up in a distant suburb of a small city in sparsely populated Australia. Driving out of the airport at home was only as complicated as choosing the right exit. She was therefore utterly unprepared for the scale of Los Angeles, and for the vehicle she'd have to command.

'That's not a car, that's a tank,' she said nervously to Jock, staring at the massive vehicle. She'd been tricked by its description as a mid-sized SUV. Compared to her old Corolla, it was a gleaming behemoth, with a confusing array of buttons, a bonnet like a cruise ship, and blind spots down both sides. It took her ten minutes to establish the handbrake was actually a foot brake, cunningly hidden down near her left leg.

'Yeah, but a tank with power steering,' Jock had said, patting her shoulder.

His reassurance did nothing to help. Mallory was thrown by the smoothness of the ride, the cushy seats that swallowed her, and the overly responsive brakes.

Then there was the right-hand driving.

Everything was backwards, and she experienced flashes of terror every time her subconscious took over and thought she was on the wrong side. This led to swerving, corrective swerving, and jamming on the brakes.

Before they'd even exited the parking lot, she'd flung all three of her passengers forward in their seatbelts. Ernie, folded into the front-passenger seat on account of his long legs, gave her sidelong stink-eye glances and pointedly hung on to the over-window handle. Jock was more patient, a calming voice from the seat behind that said, take it slow, and she would get the hang of it, and joking that at least they knew the anti-lock brakes worked. Zadie's only input was a soft, 'Whee!' after one sudden stop, as if she was on a rollercoaster.

Out on the roads, the traffic was intense, no doubt accepting all kinds of help from the volcano. Mallory drove hunched forward, her knuckles blanched around the wheel, her jaw clamping tighter with each word out of Ernie's mouth.

'You've missed a turn,' he complained for the third time.

'Don't worry, the GPS will work it out,' Mallory said.

'We're just going in circles. At this rate, we'll be in Nashville next month.'

Finally, by some miracle, they reached a freeway, and Mallory negotiated the on-ramp, trying to merge with a tiny gap in the frightening traffic. God, it was like the freeway scene in that *Matrix* movie, except she didn't have superpowers to save her. Still, she could fit . . . just another second. Then, she could relax.

'Merge!' shouted Ernie. 'Merge, merge!'

Startled, Mallory saw too late that the on-ramp had smoothly morphed into an off-ramp. She slipped back and lost her spot, left with no choice but to sail off the freeway again, and into another gridlocked garden of traffic lights. She pulled up with a jerk, her heart thumping, fingers shaking.

'Wonderful. Here we are. Again,' Ernie said.

Tears prickled on Mallory's eyelids. They were doomed to drive in circles forever. Ernie was going on and on about timetables, and how paper maps were the only proper way to navigate, and now he was playing around with the GPS, losing the route, and Jock was telling him to leave it alone. When Mallory saw a service station, she swung in and jerked to a stop.

Ernie looked up. 'Why are you stop—'

'I need to concentrate,' she said, trying to keep her voice under control. 'I'm trying to drive a strange car on these . . . these—' she waved a hand out at the long lines of brake lights '—*bloody* roads.'

'Well, I wouldn't have agreed to this if I'd known you wouldn't be able to *drive*.'

Jock laid a calming hand on Mallory's arm, climbed out and hauled Ernie's door open. 'Time to swap, Ern,' he said. 'GPS needs fixing.'

That's not all that needs fixing, Mallory muttered in her mind, then felt guilty. She prided herself on being able to connect with difficult residents, and there were many of them: people in varying stages of dementia, with hearing loss, with painful chronic conditions that made them grumpy. Or simply those who were lonely and fed up with what life had become, who even wanted to die. She felt a grave responsibility to make their lives better. She resolved to try harder.

Just as soon as they were out of the city.

It took twenty minutes to reach another on-ramp and be properly on their way. Having Jock in the front was an improvement, but it didn't stop Ernie. Should they be in the right lane? What was that the GPS just said? Could they have the radio on to see if there was a traffic update? No, Zadie didn't like the music, turn it off.

Mallory sweated, her shoulders cramped from the tension. The clock showed it was after two before they were climbing up through dry foothills out of the LA valley. She tried to count this as progress and to relax. It looked a lot like Australia, really, when you went away from the coast. Scrub-covered hills, dry earth, and big, big sky . . . and even bigger trucks.

Then they crested the mountain, and Mallory gazed all the way down the pale ribbon road, which vanished into vast plains and distant smoky blue mountains. She wasn't in Australia anymore, and it dawned on her how vast this journey might be. She gulped, feeling all that distance as a yawning space in her chest, swallowing up her courage. Maybe she should have waited in the terminal.

But Harry was out there, on the other side of it all.

'What were you going to do if you hadn't found me?' she asked, her voice trembling. 'Were you going to drive all this way on your own?'

'Nope,' Jock said, 'this is plan C.'

'Plan A was to fly, right?'

'Yes, but certain volcanoes had other ideas. I jumped on the car bookings as soon as I had reception on the tarmac. Knew they'd go fast.'

'So that makes this plan B, doesn't it?'

In the back, Ernie snorted.

'Not exactly,' Jock said. 'Plan B was Fiona. Nice lass from a contract agency.'

'She wasn't,' Ernie argued.

'Yes, she was from an agency, Ernie,' Zadie put in.

'I mean she wasn't nice.'

Jock gave Mallory a grin.

'Was that the Fiona you asked me to check the Ladies' for?' Mallory asked, as she tried to work out the cruise-control buttons.

'That's her. She joined us in Brisbane, but seems she found greener pastures in LA. Left us in the lurch. I think the lure of Hollywood might have been too strong – don't you think, Ern?' Jock said. 'We ran into you at just the right moment.'

'Took our money is what she did,' Ernie growled. 'Hollywood can have her.'

'Wait, she abandoned you in the airport?' Mallory said, aghast. 'Why would someone do that?'

After an uncomfortable pause, Jock said, 'Do you want to explain, Ernie?'

Mallory glanced in the rear-view. Zadie had drifted off, and Ernie was busy wedging a rolled-up jumper against the window as a pillow for her.

'Ern?' Jock repeated. 'Care to shed some light on Fiona's departure?'

'Nothing to do with me,' he said, his voice rough and petulant. Clearly something had happened between Ernie and the mercurial Fiona. Mallory gave Jock an enquiring eyebrow, wondering whether to worry.

'Let's just say there was a . . . personality clash,' Jock said.

Well, that was hardly surprising. Ernie was a tough customer, but this was only for a few days. Mallory finally found the cruise setting, and eased her aching right foot off the pedal. 'Well, she'll end up with a horrible reputation at her agency, that's all I'll say. They'll never give her work again.'

'She probably won't care, if she's in the next Bond flick,' Jock said.

'Bond is British,' Ernie grumbled.

Jock chuckled. 'So, how long have you worked at Silky Oaks?'

'Nearly seven years,' Mallory said. 'I started just after I left school.'

'Pity you didn't have the chance to do something more with yourself,' Ernie said.

'Geez, Ern,' Jock said.

'What? I'm just saying it's not the sort of job a young person chooses to do if they don't have to. Didn't you want to go to university? Didn't have the grades, I suppose.'

Mallory's hands reflexively tightened on the steering wheel, not just because of the question, but also because it thrust her back into that time. Her life had changed so fast in that year after school. One moment, she'd been a happy, carefree teenager, dreaming about all the one-days she'd have. Then came Duncan, being bowled over by love, wanting to support his dreams, and then she had a baby and needed to keep a roof over all their heads.

She took a deep breath. She didn't regret any of it, but neither did she want someone to think she was stupid. She'd had enough judgement from her mother and friends, and Mrs Crawley. 'Actually, I did just fine in school. But I had a baby to support. That didn't leave much room for university. I'll go one day, maybe.'

Ernie grunted. 'Pity that you had to work. Babies need their mothers. Women understood that when I was growing up. Everyone thinks they have to go back to work these days. A little economy is all that's needed.'

Mallory ground her molars. Don't rise, she thought. He's just from an older generation. But another part of her wanted to yell at him that, yes, she hadn't wanted to go to work so soon either, but she hadn't had much choice. 'Economy' didn't go far when you were the only one earning the money.

Instead, she said, 'I love my work.'

'That's really something,' Jock said. 'Not many people can say that, don't you think, Ern?'

'I suppose that's good,' he said grudgingly, but turned to stare out the window. 'You see those trees? The First Lady in sixty-five was responsible for that. Billboards were popping up all over the place, real eyesores they were. So they passed the Highway Beautification Act. Planting trees and shrubs instead. Real vision, that was, in a time where commercialism wasn't so all-consuming. Now, there's a museum—'

As Ernie kept up a patter of highway trivia from the sixties, Mallory tuned out. It was like listening to a schoolteacher. She sighed, trying to ease the muscle aches in her shoulders and arms from gripping the wheel. Only when she realised Ernie had been silent for ten minutes did she sneak a look in the rear-view. She found him asleep, catching flies with his head lolled against the seatbelt.

She blew out a long breath. 'What a day,' she said, rubbing her neck.

'You did well back there.'

She glanced across at Jock. He sat very upright in his seat, his hands resting on his knees, like he was in the front row of a school photo. The brim of his fishing hat was flipped up. 'Thanks,' she said.

'Ernie can be opinionated.'

'Mmm.' Mallory sighed, weary. She didn't want to talk about Ernie, she just wanted to put the miles between her and LA. The road slipped by, cutting a path through the pale, sandy earth of the plain. 'Sure is dry out there.'

'Oh, this is nothing. You wait till Arizona and New Mexico. It's all desert.'

'You've been here before?'

He paused. 'Not for a long time. How are you feeling? Tired?'

'Okay at the moment. That coffee must be kicking in.'

'I'll catch some shut-eye then. But wake me up if you're drooping.'

Soon, the miles were passing to a soundtrack of soft snores.

•

For two hours, she drove across the flat expanse of Apple Valley. Jock didn't sleep long, waking in time to say, 'Last chance for Vegas,' at the turn for the Interstate 40. Mallory finally felt as though they were making progress.

Ernie woke a half-hour after that, launching into serious scrutiny of a highway map he'd bought in the airport, crumpling and twisting the sheet, and muttering. This went on for what seemed like eternity before he suddenly gripped her seat from behind.

'Take this exit,' he said. His hand shot into view, pointing.

'Why?'

'Take it, take it!'

Mallory heard his apparent panic, hooked right and duly took it. The sinking sun cut through her side window, blinding her, and they bounced on the rough shoulder, pulling up down the slip-road with a wheel skid. She twisted round. 'What do you need? Are you in pain? Need the bathroom?'

Ernie sat back, pointing his good hand down the road. No sign of a medical emergency. In fact, he looked rather satisfied. 'Keep going this way now. There's something I want to show Zadie up ahead.'

Mallory pressed her hand over her still thumping heart and glanced at Jock. They'd covered so much ground, why deviate now?

'Maybe we should make a stop,' Jock said diplomatically. 'We can loop back to the interstate and find our overnight port afterwards.'

'That's what I'm saying, we can stop down here. Great place. You'll see it soon,' Ernie said.

Mallory's doubts grew the further they drove. A few tiny towns passed by, handfuls of squat buildings the same colour as the sand. Off the highway, the whole area seemed dreadfully remote. But Ernie had noticeably changed, a small-boy kind of excitement colouring his voice. He kept patting Zadie's arm and saying, 'Do you remember this, Zadie? All this desert? We stopped here, do you remember?'

Zadie looked out the window with her fingers pressed to her chin, a smile echoing the youthful version of her face in their wedding photo. 'Yes,' she said softly, at shortening intervals.

Finally, in the distance, a sign appeared, rising up like a beacon from the flat, grey-yellow desert. It was a block of black, with a big wedge of red, shaped like a sideways mouse cursor. Yellow letters announced *Roy's* with *Motel Café* vertically underneath.

But much like Mallory's cottage, the impressiveness of the sign diminished on approach. The paint was dull and peeling, the neon unlit. She pulled off the road into an empty service station. She could see a cluster of pale blue cottages and a glass-fronted building with a few crowning palm trees, but no sign of activity.

'What on earth is this?' she asked.

'*This* is a cultural icon,' Ernie huffed. 'It's a perfect example of mid-century Googie architecture.'

'Google what now?' Mallory said. She was so beyond tired, her eyes as sore as her heart, and she had no idea what Ernie was talking about.

He didn't answer. He pushed his door open and was soon encouraging Zadie out of her seat. The two of them were halfway across the dusty lot, heading for the café, before Mallory could even work out if the place was open. She peered at some construction fencing in the distance. Down the way, a group of bikers were taking photos. It was kind of creepy.

Jock caught her eye across the cab. 'Did you ever see *Psycho*?'

Mallory shuddered. 'I hate scary movies, but I've seen enough of them to know that the desperate carload of people looking for a place to stay shouldn't stay here.'

To say she hated scary movies was an understatement. Duncan was the one who enjoyed them. He used to trot out gems like *Friday the 13th* and *Scream* and the original *A Nightmare on Elm Street*, scoffing popcorn while Mallory hid under a blanket. She'd been scarred for life just watching the opening sequence of *The Ring*. The music still induced palpitations. Duncan used to dig her face out of the blanket and kiss her on the nose, wrapping his arms around her. 'Come on, watch it, it'll be good for you,' he'd said.

Mallory, feeling fragile as the high notes of a horror soundtrack dug fingers into her nightmares, used to turn her face into his chest until it was over.

She'd been mildly horrified when Harry seemed to have inherited Duncan's inclinations. He loved creepy-crawlies and haunted houses and Halloween, and giggled delightedly when scared. He wielded the bug catcher, marching in to tame lurking shower spiders and release them safely outside, his hair flopping forward as he crouched, watching them scurry off all bandy-legged into the undergrowth. Mallory watched with less fascination, sure each spared arachnid was plotting an immediate return inside, and trying not to think of the shower scene in *Arachnophobia*. The only safe release was directly under the heel of her shoe, John Candy-style . . . if only she wasn't so squeamish about it.

Now, looking about this dusty place, the over-large beat-up road sign made her think of a deep-sea angler fish, luring prey in the dark with a big shiny light. She only knew about angler fish because of Harry. She could see him, poring over a book of undersea creatures, which all resembled the monster from *Alien*.

So lost was she in that image of him that, as she climbed out of the car, she expected Harry to erupt from the back seat and go hurtling across the dust, shouting, 'Mum! Come on! Awesome!'

It wasn't until Jock said, 'Got that right,' that she crashed back into reality. She couldn't even remember what they'd been talking about. Ripping Harry's phantom presence away was enough to knock her breath out. He *wasn't* here. Her little boy was still down that endless road.

I'm coming, baby.

Mallory started as her phone rang. After fumbling the handset in the hope it was Harry, she saw instead a familiar number.

'This volcano is all over the news!' Bridget said, sounding very far away. 'I thought you might be stuck in the airport. Nothing's flying over the US.'

'I was stuck, but I managed to make other plans,' Mallory said, her eyes following two tiny dust devils whirling across the cracked pavement. 'I'm driving.'

'What? All that way?'

'It was that, or go home,' Mallory said, into the crackling line. The connection really was awful.

'Aye,' Bridget said, after a pause. 'I suppose desperate times and all that. I just wanted to know you were okay, and that I'll tell Crawley you had a family emergency.'

'Oh, thank you! I owe you one, Bridge.' Mallory had meant to call work, but with her rapid departure and the whole ash-cloud thing, she'd forgotten. That was all she needed: to come back and find she'd been fired.

'Nothing owed. Just stay safe, okay, duckie? I'll call you later.'

Mallory closed her eyes and let herself slump against the car, her forehead on her arm. Fatigue was setting hard in her bones. Only the jet lag was propping her eyelids open like broken vertical blinds. And yet all she wanted to do was slide into the driver's seat and keep going.

'Hey, Mallory.'

'Mmm?'

Jock was peering at her with concern. 'We'd better call it a day I think. I'll grab a sandwich for you and we'll round up Ernie and Zade, and find somewhere to stay, okay?'

After Ernie's enthusiasm for mid-century architecture, Mallory anticipated the rounding up would take some time. Ernie, however, was already on his way back, red-faced, though Zadie seemed fresher than the long journey should have allowed, as if this place really was a fond memory.

'Been a few changes since we were last here,' Ernie said, grumpy. 'Hotel's closed. Being restored, apparently.'

'When exactly were you last here?' Jock asked.

A pause. 'Nineteen sixty-eight.'

Jock chuckled.

Under a bruised purple sunset, Mallory drove the SUV back into the desert. The sun was well behind the distant low hills, throwing long shadows towards the night. The road out here was lonely, so Mallory minded less that Ernie talked nonstop as they drove.

'Course, the interstates stripped the life out of the old sixty-six, that's why hard-working businesses like that have just died. Such a shame. No one appreciates these things until they're gone.'

'And yet curious how that interstate is also going to allow us to thwart the volcano, and reach Nashville in four days. How about appreciating that,' Jock said.

'That's hardly the point. It's commercialisation at its worst, the scourge of innovative business.' Ernie returned to scrutinising his map, a pair of bifocals pushed down his nose.

'Didn't think you were such a fan of innovation,' Jock said mildly.

'Just stay on this road,' Ernie said, and then continued to report the same at intervals.

Eventually, Jock looked around. 'We do have a GPS, Ern,' he said, pointing to the unit.

'Don't trust it. What if the satellites go down?'

'What if that map you're using was printed in nineteen sixty-eight?' Jock shot back.

Just when Mallory was wishing that both of them would find a mute button, her phone rang again. Hoping it might be Harry, she threw all thoughts of serial killers out the window and pulled onto the shoulder, slipping to put on the foot brake while she groped for the phone, which encouragingly said 'private number'. The car's engine hummed in time with Ernie's grumble as she pressed talk.

'Hello?'

'Ah, Mallory.'

Mallory's heart flopped into the asphalt. She screwed her eyes shut and grimaced. 'Hi . . . Mrs Crawley.'

'I had you on the roster this morning, but Bridget tells me you have a family emergency. How late will you be?'

'Oh, yes . . . you see, the thing is that I had to fly to America. And then this volcano happened. Actually, it's funny, you'll never guess who I ran into. Three residents—hey!'

Mallory's phone flew away from her face, and collected the dash with a thud.

'Jesus, Ernie,' Jock exclaimed. 'Was that really necessary?'

Mallory peered around to find Ernie with his cane raised. What the . . . *had he just knocked the phone out of her hand?*

'What was *that* for?' she demanded. 'You could have hit me in the head!' She retrieved the handset from the floor. Remarkably, the phone seemed intact but Mrs Crawley was gone.

Zadie leaned forward, eyebrows knitted in concern. 'Are you all right, Mabel?'

'I think so,' Mallory said doubtfully. She straightened up only because Jock had confiscated Ernie's cane.

'She was going to tell Crawley,' Ernie said, arms folded.

'What on earth is the problem?' For the first time in this misadventure, Mallory trembled. She was out here, miles from help, with three people she hardly knew, one of whom was a cheap paperback page away from behaving like a lunatic. She stared at the three of them, willing someone to speak.

After a short pause, Jock said, 'Are you going to tell her, or will I? She should probably know, Ern.'

'Tell me what?'

'Keep driving,' Ernie said, sitting back. 'We all need some dinner. Then, we'll talk.'

•

It didn't take long to find the interstate, and Mallory swung the SUV east, the atmosphere so tense she could have played a tune on the air coming from the vents. An hour later, they reached the town of Needles, tucked into the side of the Colorado River. Under a blanket of stars, the main street presented a cheerful array of motels. Jock pointed to one and Mallory pulled in. Fifteen minutes later, the four of them were sitting in the next-door diner, complete with cherry-red booth seats, chrome-stemmed bar stools, and checked napkins. An attentive waitress wore a yellow uniform dress with a white apron, her thick blonde hair caught up in a bouncy ponytail. Mallory felt as if she'd walked onto a movie set, in a scene where the nefarious plan is laid out.

Ernie studied the menu for five long minutes before ordering an omelette to share with Zadie – no onions, no peppers, no chilli, extra cheese, not too hot. Jock ordered a cheeseburger and fries. Mallory ordered the same, because it was the first thing she saw, before pushing her menu away. She kept an eye on Ernie's cane, which he'd stowed on the chair back between the booths.

Finally, the waitress pushed her pen behind her ear. 'All right. Now you just sit back and relax, and I'll take care of everything,' she said with an energy that to Mallory was a dim memory.

'Nice girl,' Jock said.

Mallory shifted her gaze between him and Ernie, and Ernie's cane, and Zadie – who was laying out her animal photographs like cards in Solitaire.

'I guess I'll start.' Jock leaned forward. 'You see, we didn't exactly leave Silky Oaks with permission. That's why Ernie didn't want Crawley to know where we are.'

Mallory, mid-yawn, instantly woke. 'What? You mean, you just—'

'Walked out? Yeah, pretty much.'

cultivated a friendship with one of the gardeners, who came around the rear door plant boxes at the same time each day and who, for a quiet fifty slipped into a pocket, was quite happy to pick them all up in one of the golf-carts and ferry them down to the street. From there, they'd taken an Uber to the airport – because Jock suspected Silky Oaks might call taxi companies – where they'd met up with the now-departed Fiona. Ernie chipped in with all the places the plot had nearly come undone, until he was actually smiling, and Mallory was laughing at the audacity of their plan.

Even Zadie was grinning. They could have all been twenty, living up the first day of a road trip. Finally, with the table covered in plates and trays and napkins, Mallory was yawning. Ernie and Jock had both slumped, Ernie with his arm around Zadie, who was slowly sliding the trays into each other, and stacking the plates and napkins.

'You don't have to do that!' exclaimed the waitress, who came back to clear the table and ask if they wanted pie, which they all declined.

Finally, when they were alone again, Jock said, 'Are you going to turn us in?'

Mallory shook her head. 'But I should still call them. Someone should know where you are; someone other than me, I mean.'

'No calls,' Ernie said. 'We have insurance if there's a problem.'

'What does it matter? They can't stop you now.'

'Did you have to tell your landlord where you were going before you left home?' Jock asked.

'No . . .' Mallory conceded. 'But then I didn't pay off the gardener to escape either.'

Jock grinned. 'Fair point. But the rulebook is pretty thick on unauthorised travel. They could probably give away our rooms and stuff. This way, we'll be back before they can put anything in motion.'

'They wouldn't do that,' Mallory started, but then stopped, because she wasn't quite sure. The contracts that residents signed were long and complicated. Who knew what Silky Oaks might be able to do in this situation? Besides, her main concern was reaching New York and finding Harry. Everything else was secondary.

Later, Jock pulled her aside when she came out of the bathroom.

'Look,' he said, 'I'll call Silky Oaks, let them know we're okay and to call off any searches. Just tell Ernie what he wants to hear.'

Mallory nodded. She wanted to end this, needed to sleep; they all did. Either way, she knew she would keep driving tomorrow. So she went back to the table. 'Here, I'll take my SIM card out if it makes you feel better,' she said. She would be temporarily unreachable to Mrs Crawley, but she didn't want to finish that conversation now, and she had the wi-fi at the motel should Harry call.

With Ernie satisfied, they stepped outside into the night, walking the short path between the diner and the motel. Mallory swayed on her feet. Ernie was patting his pockets.

'Can't find the keys,' he said.

'Car keys or room keys?'

'Both.'

Several confused minutes followed of trying to establish where they'd last been seen, until Ernie remembered Zadie had been holding them at the diner.

And that was how Mallory ended up, jet lagged to the teeth, digging through a dumpster near the California–Arizona border. The waitress was sympathetic, bringing a flashlight and helping her pull out the bags.

'You must be exhausted,' she said, after Mallory had told her how far they'd all travelled in the past two days. 'Still, it's real sweet taking your grandparents on a road trip.'

Mallory found the room keys sandwiched between two slices of buttered toast, and the car keys buried in a scrunched napkin.

When she arrived back at the motel, she was shaking with a level of exhaustion she hadn't experienced since Harry was a tiny baby, and she still needed to help Zadie and Ernie change. When she finally went back to her room and fell into bed, it hit her: they'd only driven five hours today, and Jock had told her it was forty hours to Nashville.

Chapter 6

THE NEXT MORNING, MALLORY WOKE TO ERNIE BANGING on the door with his cane, needing help with the bathroom. She stumbled out, disoriented and groggy, and only just managed to do her job. She was so tired, and could have gone back to bed for hours. Jock was the one who saved her, wordlessly pushing a coffee into her hands. He looked far too spry for yesterday's adventures, already showered and dressed, fishing hat in place.

They were on the road again by seven. Mallory spent the first hour rubbing sleep from her eyes and squinting into the bright sun, which rimmed the distant clouds in fluorescent orange.

'Volcanic sunrise,' Jock said, turning on the radio. The news was full of the ash cloud, the airport chaos, and speculation about how long it might all last. Out here, in the sands of the Mojave Desert with its pale earth and vaulted sky, the drama seemed to be taking place in a parallel universe.

Mallory's jet lag, which felt like stuffing in her head, added to the disconnection, but at least they were moving. Zadie especially was having a good day, asking if Mallory had eaten breakfast, and what type of music she liked to listen to.

Mallory stammered halfway through an answer before Ernie interrupted and asked Jock to hook up his phone to the car radio. Soon, *The Eagles' Greatest Hits* was flowing through the speakers.

'I didn't think when I helped you digitise this stuff that I'd have to listen to it,' Jock said, twisting in his seat as 'Take It Easy' began.

Ernie folded his arms. 'What's wrong with The Eagles?'

'What's right with The Eagles?' Jock said, but he was grinning as if this was a friendly argument they'd had before.

'I never liked their music much,' Zadie said, her voice high and clear. 'But Don Henley was a dish.'

'Who's Don Henley?' Mallory asked.

'He played guitar,' Zadie said. 'And he's a conservationist. Do you know the Walden Woods Project?'

'What's that?'

'It's a woodland in Massachusetts,' Ernie cut in. 'Thoreau stayed in a cabin there, and it inspired his book *Walden*. Wonderful story about self-reliance, and simplicity, and that progress isn't everything. Real piece of classic literature. You must have heard of it?'

Mallory didn't even dare ask who Thoreau was. Instead, she caught Zadie's eye in the rear-view. 'You sound very community-minded,' she said, hoping to encourage her.

'Oh, yes,' Ernie said proudly. 'Zadie was an accomplished nurse for many years, and she was a hugely successful fundraiser for charities – hospitals, the RSPCA, homeless shelters. All in her twenties, mind you. She really had the drive to achieve.'

In the pause that followed, Mallory couldn't help feel the implied judgement in Ernie's tone, the contrast of this drive to achieve and her own failures. She did her best to brush it off.

'And is that how you met? At work?' she asked.

'In a way. I went to Nashville in sixty-eight for a conference at Vanderbilt University,' he said. 'Zadie was volunteering at a missionary training college nearby – it had the most lovely grounds. I walked in there one day when it was pouring rain to find shelter, and there she was.'

'Your coat was all dark on the shoulders. From the rain,' Zadie said.

'Yes, that's right. You remember, love?'

'Dr King spoke in the chapel,' Zadie said, the gentle lilt of her southern accent coming through. 'I crept in the back to hear. Daddy was ever so cross.'

'Dr King?' Mallory asked, curious. 'You mean, Martin Luther King?'

'Wonderful Christian man,' Zadie said. 'My father didn't like him much.'

'King did speak there,' Ernie said quickly, 'but that was years before we met, Zade. That was when you were maybe seven years old. I'm talking about after we met, and I'd planned to drive back to Los Angeles. You remember that? I'd bought a car to see the Main Street of America. Zadie had never left Nashville and wanted to go. The rest is history.'

Nineteen sixty-eight. Mallory calculated.

'Fifty years together. That's really something,' she said, trying to comprehend it. That was such a long time, and there must have been ups and downs. Could she and Duncan ever have had that long together? 'Are you going back to visit family now?' Mallory asked.

'We're going to a wedding,' Zadie said with excitement.

'Oh lovely. And—'

'I think that's enough on that,' Ernie said firmly. 'Mallory doesn't need to know our business.'

Mallory sighed as the conversation again derailed. Just when she thought she was getting somewhere. Rounded hills flanked the highway, crowned with green shrubs, and underneath the now overcast sky the desert seemed less forbidding than it did in the open sun. But time went so slowly in silence.

She rubbed her neck, stiff from too little sleep. *Three more days.*

'How old is your little boy?' Zadie asked abruptly.

Mallory dropped her hand and glanced in the rear-view, surprised Zadie remembered. 'He's five.'

'And what's his name?'

'Harry.'

Zadie made an approving sound in her throat. 'Lovely traditional name, don't you think, Ernie?'

'Mallory said yesterday,' Ernie said. 'I was saying how it's a dreadful shame how mothers have to work these days. They don't have any time with their babies when they're young.'

Mallory clamped her teeth, and very slowly sucked a breath. She knew she shouldn't rise, but holding in a rebuttal only intensified her heartache.

'Ernie's an obstetrician,' Jock said quickly. 'He's got opinions on these things.'

'And why shouldn't I? No one thinks about the children. It's all *me, me, me* with young people, handing off their little ones to strangers.'

'I did think about it, actually,' Mallory said tightly. 'I worked a lot of community night shifts so I could be there during the day, and my husband looked after him when I couldn't. I didn't *hand him off* to anyone.'

Ernie paused. 'Your husband? Oh, I see.'

Only then did it dawn on Mallory that Ernie must have assumed she had been an irresponsible teenager who'd got herself pregnant and been forced to abandon her child into care. And worse, he'd judged her for it.

'Yes, my husband,' she said. 'Not that it matters, but Harry never went to childcare for a single day ... at least, not until this past year. In fact, he's with my husband in New York right now.'

No need to mention the circumstances. He could stuff his opinions.

'I see,' Ernie said stiffly. 'I do apologise if I had a different impression. I suppose you must have worked very hard.'

Mallory wondered if he had a mild superpower for turning compliments into backhanders, or if he just didn't believe her. After all, if her husband was in New York and expecting her, why would she have been stuck in LA without any cash?

'And how about you, Jock?' Mallory asked, hoping to prevent Ernie reaching any conclusions. 'Are you going to this wedding too?'

'Me? No.' He hesitated. 'I'm going straight on from there.'

'Where to?'

Again, hesitation. 'Further north.' Jock tapped his fingers against his knee and reached for the GPS. 'To visit my brother.'

'Where's he live?'

Another pause. 'Virginia. It's a fair drive on after Nashville.'

Hearing his obvious reluctance, Mallory let the subject drop.

'Tell you what though, Zadie,' Jock said a minute later. 'Pretty progressive for the sixties, young woman like you upping and leaving with a man, even if he was a doctor.'

'She was eighteen,' Ernie said.

'Just. Her passport said she was born in nineteen-fifty.'

Mallory glanced in the rear-view. The muscle in Ernie's jaw quilted. 'I'll thank you not to abuse privileged information,' he said.

'Passport's hardly privileged information. Especially when I helped you get it.'

'Not how I see it. You don't exactly have the authority to—'

'Oh, listen, this one's a classic,' Mallory said, pouncing to turn up the music as 'Hotel California' came on. In fact, she rather hated the song, with its mournful melody and depressing lyrics, but anything to head off a conflict. She'd learned distraction techniques with Harry. After yesterday's incident, she'd insisted on Ernie stowing his cane in the boot, but the last thing she wanted was septuagenarian fisticuffs in a moving vehicle.

After a few seconds, Jock resumed poking at the GPS. 'Sorry,' he said.

Mallory rubbed her forehead, feeling cooped up in the car. 'Let's just make it to the next stop without blows, okay?'

The road ran on across a vast plain where train tracks scribed great arcs, sometimes touching the line of the road before diving off on a different curve into the distance. Triple and quadruple locos pulled double-decker container cars along the lines. Harry had been single-minded about trains since the age of two. Mallory could imagine him pressed up against the window, counting the wagons and calling out the numbers on the engines, and asking to stop to witness the big diesels thundering past.

She hadn't spoken to him in forty-eight hours. Please, she thought, let this drive be flawless. Let me reach him and fast.

•

For a while, they settled into a predictable rhythm for the journey, driving through shifting scenery while listening to a cycle of nostalgic songs and radio news, and then eating roadside food. Rinse and repeat.

Flagstaff, Arizona, flew past within the hour, bringing a landscape of elevated hills and pine forest bright with spring foliage. One mountain even had a snow cap. Then the mountain was in the rear-view, and the plains opened up again, pale green grass stretching from one horizon to the other, the wind rippling the surface like water.

Ernie again grumbled about the interstate, that it cut across the continent, barely touching down anywhere, but Mallory was only too happy to be a skipping stone.

After three hours, they stopped at a lonely petrol station with a Dairy Queen, and Mallory stretched her legs before they sat down to an early lunch. The TV screens were filled with volcano news.

'What exactly is that?' she asked, when Jock dug into a plate of unidentifiable white lumps in a white sauce, with a brown crumble on top.

He scratched his head. 'Biscuits and gravy with sausage, allegedly,' he said. 'It was this, or fifteen different varieties of sugar and peanut butter. Take your pick.' He emptied out a shopping bag loaded with Nutter Butters, Twinkies, Oreos, cheese-filled pretzels, Red Vines, chips, and numerous other glossy foil packets. Ernie frowned his disapproval.

Mallory pushed the packets around and chose one without really looking at it. She wanted to keep driving. After she'd helped Zadie and Ernie to the bathroom, they were nearly back to the car when Jock tapped Mallory on the shoulder.

'Here,' he said, holding out a pair of sunglasses, new tags still dangling off them. 'You were squinting something awful, and we're going to be driving east every morning. Also, I'm sorry about what Ernie said. Don't let him get to you. He's really an okay guy.'

'Thanks,' she said, but she still couldn't help feeling judged and inadequate in Ernie's eyes. It shouldn't have bothered her – after all, she'd encountered dozens of prickly residents over her time at Silky Oaks – but something about Ernie chafed her. Mallory found herself oddly protective of Zadie, and wondered how the two of them could suit each other.

'One more thing.' Jock held out a credit-card sized packet. 'I have a spare phone card. Please take it. Number's on the back. If you were roaming with your Australian one, it'll bankrupt you and you'll need a phone after Nashville. This has data and calls. Assuming you can get reception anywhere out here.'

Mallory was so touched by his kindness, she nearly cried. 'Aren't you worried I'll call Silky Oaks?' she said.

He shrugged. 'Just don't mention it to Ernie, okay?'

Mallory slid the glasses on with a sigh of relief and prepared to drive on, but found Ernie pondering his map, which he'd spread on the car's bonnet and weighted down with his cane. He had a yellowing photograph in his hand.

'I recognise this road,' he said, pointing across to a narrow bitumen strip alongside the interstate.

'All looks the same to me,' she said. 'Shall we go?'

'Look here,' Ernie said, poking the photo under her nose. 'Look at the shape of these hills, that double bump over there.'

Mallory peered at the faded image, and had to admit it did look like the same place. Maybe.

'We stopped here in sixty-eight, I'm sure of it,' said Ernie. 'There's an Indian trading post down there.'

'Doesn't look like anything's down there but tumbleweeds and potholes,' Mallory said, squinting down the tiny road.

'Believe me, it's there,' Ernie insisted as she climbed back into the car. 'Go that way.'

'I don't want to get lost.'

'We can't get lost with that GP-whatsit. The road will join up with the highway again, just a bit further down. Genuine Indian trading post.'

'Selling genuine stuff made in China and Mexico?' Jock said, then as Ernie scowled. 'I'm joking, Ern. Maybe we should just stick to the interstate.'

'I'm telling you this was a proper place with handcrafted goods. Zadie loved it. Be good for her to see it again. Help her memory.'

'I bought a poncho,' Zadie said from the back seat. 'A purple one. With all these squares of black and white.'

Ernie beamed with pure love.

As Mallory took the turn she wasn't happy, but consoled herself that she could still see the interstate. It was right there, across a strip of grassy land, and Jock offered the further comfort that the GPS indeed showed a highway entry only a few miles away.

'After that, it's an hour and a half to Holbrook,' he said. 'Probably stop there tonight, or a little further if you're okay to push on.'

When the sun vanished behind a cloud, she slid the glasses up on her head. On this narrow service road, the vast ocean of shifting grasses grew taller, as if the car was slowly sinking beneath the fronds. The gusting wind tumbled through the grass heads and buffeted the windows. Mallory frowned. That felt like storm winds. Sure enough, when she glanced out Jock's window, she saw a graphite smudge on the southern horizon. Her stomach flipped in a familiar and unpleasant way.

'What's that?' she said in a small voice, pointing.

Jock peered out. 'Looks like weather.'

'A storm?'

'Miles away,' Ernie said from the back. 'Moving slow.'

'Not necessarily a good thing,' Jock said. 'If it moves fast, it's gone fast.'

'Arizona is the lightning death capital of America,' put in Zadie. 'The guide book said so.'

'Great,' muttered Mallory. Why did it have to be a storm? She had visions of the unearthly patterns lightning made on the walls at home, when thunder cracked like splintering bones, and sticks whipped down on the roof. At home she could barely function with that going on, and here they were out in the open.

'What did I say – look!' Ernie said, pulling her back to the present.

A squat white building had appeared ahead. Mallory prepared to eat her words, until they came close enough to see the signs of abandonment. She pulled the car across the broken tarmac of the parking lot, weeds growing tall through the cracks. The building's white walls were yellowed by time and sun, windows smashed into stars.

Ernie was quiet as he climbed out and limped across. Mallory followed. Through one broken window, she could see empty tables and rafters full of cobwebs. A lonely, chipped buffalo figurine lay on its side on the floor, and an unidentifiable heap of fabric – perhaps ponchos made in Mexico – was piled in a corner. Not even Jock said anything.

'I'm sorry, Ernie,' Mallory said.

She did feel sorry for him, standing there before the tumbledown building, his expectations soured into disappointment for a second time. But if he felt such things, he didn't betray them, simply limped back to the car with a shake of his head. Mallory could hear him apologising to Zadie, and she in return patted his arm, the universal signal for *it doesn't matter*, though Ernie obviously thought it did. Mallory almost wished the place had been open, just to see Ernie smile.

Five minutes later, they were back in the car, pulling onto the service road with The Eagles still softly playing. After ten minutes, the road was still narrowing, the pavement cracked and lumpy.

'Shouldn't we have joined back to the highway by now?' she asked, slowing as the car wheels vibrated over the surface.

Jock frowned at the GPS screen. 'We've passed the point it said there was a ramp. Maybe the map's not up to date.'

'What do we do?'

'I guess we either keep going, or we turn back.'

No way was she going back. The interstate was maddeningly close, just across that strip of land and behind its low fence. Trucks burned past at seventy-five miles an hour, making it seem as though the car was hardly moving.

Finally, Mallory spotted an overpass. 'There it is,' she said with relief and accelerated.

'Excellent.' Jock stowed the GPS and leaned back.

Then the steering wheel wobbled. Mallory eased off the accelerator, hearing an ominous *fop-fop-fop*. The wobble amplified and the car sank in the back.

She bit her lip. Please, no. That was *not* a flat tyre; not here, not now. The noise was just because of the bad road. Any second now, when they reached that ramp and its smooth concrete surface, all would be well.

Jock glanced across. 'Feels like a tyre,' he said. 'Better stop.'

Swearing under her breath at the traitorous gods of motor vehicles, Mallory pulled the car to a stop. A few seconds later, she and Jock were staring at the deflated rubber of the rear passenger tyre, slumped like black dough under the wheel rim.

'I've got pins in my back and disc problems,' Jock said apologetically. 'Should I call a roadside assist?'

'That's okay,' Mallory said, feeling the pressure of time. Better to get this over with. 'I know how to change a tyre.'

She did. Once, when she was eighteen and two months pregnant, she'd been stuck after a late shift with a flat. She'd messaged Duncan, who had taken over an hour to pick her up, by which time it was past midnight and she was nearly hysterical. He'd apologised profusely: an unmissable conference call with developers in Chicago. But Mallory had been unpleasantly reminded of her mother, who never knew how to do anything around the house, always waiting for Mallory's father to get around to it, even though he almost never did.

At the time, there'd been a male orderly at Silky Oaks called Chris who drove a vintage muscle car and proudly told anyone who would listen that he'd done it up himself. Mallory had summoned the courage to ask him at lunch.

'You don't know how to change a tyre?' he'd asked around his mouthful of sausage roll, as astonished as if she'd said she didn't know how to brush her teeth. But he'd had kindness. After their shifts, in the staff carpark, he'd taken her through changing every tyre on her car until it was burned into her muscle memory.

She'd been late home, and Duncan had been mad. 'Who's this Chris guy?' he'd asked more than once. Later, Duncan had apologised and said he only felt awful because Mallory should be able to rely on him. But Mallory liked relying on herself, and swiftly learned how to fix leaking taps, adjust door hinges, and pull hair balls and lost toys from drain holes, all critical skills for living in the cottage.

Now, she swiped away chilled sweat with the back of her forearm. She had looked after herself and Harry for the past year, and she would finish this job too. They would all be warm and dry in the next town before long, and she would be in New York before she knew it. *Positive thoughts.*

She popped the trunk, trying not to look to the south, where the storm was spreading, a purple and grey bruise on the sky.

•

Of course, knowing how to change a tyre and doing it were two completely different things. For a start, they had to remove all the luggage to search for the jack and the spare, which were hidden under the floor of the boot. And then the spare turned out to be a dreaded space saver, so they'd have to limp at low speed into the next town and have the puncture fixed before they could drive on.

'Where's the wheel brace?' Mallory said, staring at the empty cavity around the space saver. Gusts of chilly wind buffeted her as she searched, and eventually found the brace cunningly hidden in a side panel. By then, she had a gooseflesh road from neck to wrist.

She lay on the grubby bitumen, trying to push the jack into the correct position. Her face burned with stress; she must have a red-hot flush up to her earlobes.

'It says there should be two notches in the chassis,' Jock called helpfully, the owner's manual open on his lap.

Mallory finally found the spot. 'Aha!' she said, aligning the jack with grim satisfaction.

Raising the jack up was awkward and slow, but soon it was touching the chassis, and she was ready to remove the nuts. After that, she'd jack the car and have the tyre off, then new one on, all done. So much faster than waiting around for help and not a moment too soon. She was starting to feel the irrational storm terror sinking its claws into her, and was eager to reach the next town. The last thing she wanted was to embarrass herself in front of her passengers.

As she was aligning the wheel brace, she heard a distinctive galloping engine roar on the interstate. A motorbike was coming towards them from the ramp ahead, a big black and chrome machine. The rider must have turned off the wrong way, and was now rumbling to a stop.

Mallory kept working, watching from the corner of her eye. A big guy in black leather swung his leg off, spiked his helmet onto the handlebars and came towards them with ground-eating strides. Mallory felt herself shrink. What the hell did he want?

'Howdy,' he said. 'You wanna hand with that?'

Later, she reflected that he might have sounded perfectly friendly. Might have had the very best intentions. But Mallory suddenly wasn't a grown woman on the roadside in Arizona. She was a little girl, back in her mother's house, watching through a split in the curtains while a man like this walked up the overgrown path and pounded his meaty knuckles into the front door. She heard the metallic chink of the door chain, the growling voice that threatened her father about money he owed someone. She felt the *crack* of wood as the man shouldered the door so hard, the chain broke. He'd just been making a point, trying to scare her parents. A minute later, his black boots had carried him out of their yard, but that incident had scarred a deep corner of Mallory's soul.

So now, she moved her body on instinct, blocking the man out. 'No. I'm fine,' she said, her whole body braced.

He took a step back, but Mallory still felt his presence behind her like the gathering storm: big, mean, and to be fled from as fast as possible.

'Got a storm coming in,' he said. 'You see that? And I'm a mechanic.'

She snuck a look at him, his features amplified by her dread. He towered over her, black sunglasses hiding his eyes, but not the yellowing bruise spreading into his left cheek and temple. His chest was absurdly muscular under his jacket. He didn't make any move towards the tyre, but he didn't leave either. Mallory turned back to the wheel, hoping he would evaporate, like the monsters under her childhood bed who couldn't find her if her eyes were closed.

'I'm nearly done,' she lied.

'Well,' he drawled doubtfully, 'if you're sure now.'

'Perfectly, thank you.' Her words were like chips of ice.

Ernie tried to cut in. 'I think we should let this man—'

'Ernie.' Her voice shot out, sharp and clipped. 'I know how to change a damn tyre. Butt out, will you?'

With this, the biker tipped a finger at his forehead as if he were wearing a hat. 'If you folks are fine, I better go run that storm into town. All y'all take care now.'

Mallory held herself rigid until he and his overloud bike disappeared down the road. Then she heaved a breath. Her heart was thundering, her arms jelly, as if she'd just survived a robbery at gunpoint and then decided to finish off the experience with a marathon of push-ups.

She took another breath, but her heart rate refused to normalise. The brace hung heavy from her hand.

'We could have been done by now,' Ernie complained, gesturing with his good hand at the departed bike. 'Why would you turn away a competent man's help?'

Competent man, ha! 'Don't worry,' Mallory said, through her clenched teeth. 'I *do* know how to change a tyre.'

No need to flinch at the lightning flashes, or to feel this was taking too long.

She shoved against the wheel brace, channelling her frustration. Chris had never mentioned that a flat tyre could be so *hot*. She kept catching her knuckles on the scorching rim. And this second-last nut wouldn't budge, no matter how she strained against it. She shifted position, tried again, feeling like her back muscles were about to pop.

'Come on,' she growled. She stood, and leaned all her weight on the brace.

The nut gave, and she fell, her knuckles crashing into the wheel hub. She heard one of them crack, and she tumbled rather ungracefully into the side of the car.

A hand touched her shoulder. 'You hurt?' Jock said. 'Want Ernie to take a look?'

'No, no,' she said, looking up to reassure him. He was holding his hat on against the wind. 'I just slipped. A graze, that's all.'

It wasn't quite the truth. On the surface, it didn't look bad: a sliver of skin had lifted off across the middle knuckle, as fine as tissue paper. But underneath, a deep-purple bruise spread between the first and second knuckle. Nothing seemed broken; she just needed a minute to recover. She tried to make a fist, and it felt like someone was driving a knife through her hand. No way was she going to ask Ernie to look at it.

Zadie wound down her electric window. The dark clouds seemed halfway across the sky now, the front a murky shade of green, much like Mallory's knuckle would look in a few days. An icy water drop flew into Mallory's forehead.

'Mabel,' Zadie said, 'it's going to snow. Just like it did before Christmas.'

'I'm sorry this is taking so long,' Mallory told her, slowly flexing her hand.

'You hurt yourself?'

Mallory extended the hand, hiding her discomfort. 'Just a bruise, see?'

Zadie reached out, and her fingers on Mallory's skin were smooth and warm and reassuring. 'You're a brave girl,' she said.

Mallory had to look away as tears prickled her eyes. Having rebutted an offer of help she didn't want to let Zadie down. 'Thanks,' she said with a sniff. 'But it's not going to snow. We're in the middle of the desert.'

'Mallory.' Jock raised his eyes up to the sky. 'I think we'd better get moving.'

'It won't snow, right?' she asked, far less certain.

'I don't want to scare you, but four years ago there was a snow storm in April. In Flagstaff.'

Mallory tried to pull in a calming breath, but her lungs were stiff. 'Isn't that the place we just drove through?'

'The same.' He shrugged and pointed at his phone. 'Sorry. Can't help that it's all on Google.'

'Great.'

She fitted the wheel brace on the last nut, which was tight, too, refusing to shift. Some lug-nut must have done them up in a shop with a power tool. After her last experience, she applied her weight with her foot. She leaned until her other foot left the ground and she was actually standing on the brace. Uh-oh. That wasn't good. Her weight wasn't enough. Left with no options, she stomped on it.

A metallic *snap* echoed off the road as her foot met the ground again, followed by a *tink* as one part of the wheel brace landed on the asphalt, another in some nearby grass.

Mallory and Jock stared for five shocked heartbeats. The wheel brace had snapped neatly across its weld into two very useless pieces.

She lost it. 'You've got to be kidding me! This is a brand-new car! How could that even happen?'

Jock peered at the broken pieces. 'Well . . . does it say, "Made in China"?'

Chapter 7

MALLORY TRIED EVERYTHING TO FIX THE WHEEL BRACE, or at least make it usable. She lashed the pieces together with bandages from Ernie's first-aid kit, but that couldn't hold up under the torque. A belt was just as useless. Ernie searched the car for the hire agreement and the emergency numbers, before concluding that Fiona must have walked off with them. In the meantime, Jock found booking information in his records and hunched in the front seat out of the wind, mobile pressed to his ear. From the lack of conversation, Mallory concluded that there was either no reception, or he was on extended hold. No assistance was coming soon.

She trekked across the gap to the interstate to try to flag someone down. She got close enough for the trucks zooming past to nearly knock her over, and realised the road had no shoulder. Worse, while there was an entry, there was no official exit. The man on the bike had turned off the wrong way, and any other compassionate motorists were unlikely to make the backwards turn. Icy raindrops spat down. The dark clouds had banished the sun and rebuilt the desert in shades of shadow. As she stumbled back, Mallory imagined them stuck inside the crippled car while the storm thundered through. Her panic rose to horror-movie levels.

She heard an engine above the traffic then, loud, and galloping, and ten seconds later a black motorbike came into view on the other side of the highway, the rider hunched against the wind. Wait . . . was that the same bike?

As it screamed past, Mallory's hopes sank, but a minute later she heard it again, coming back towards them. He took the same illegal turn as before, gunning down the service road, and pulled up.

Desensitised after the first encounter, Mallory had a better look at him, even as the wind whipped her hair across her face. He certainly made an impression, swinging his leg off the machine, a wall of bone and muscle and leather. Raindrops made tiny explosion marks over his jacket shoulders and sunglasses. Rather like that big guy in a movie Duncan had made her watch once. A face with no expression; a machine man, out to kill.

He had parked a little further back this time, as if he wasn't sure of his reception. Then he grinned. 'Thought you said you knew how to change a tyre,' he said, his words running together in a liquid drawl of amusement.

Mallory was still holding the broken back of the wheel brace. She lifted it, as much defence as explanation. 'Well, this broke . . .' she started. Then all the fight went out of her. She was hurt and exhausted. She needed a port. 'Don't suppose you've got one of these in your Harley?' she asked.

He tipped his glasses up on his head. Beyond the ugly bruise on his face, she saw his eyes for the first time – blue, behind thick lashes. 'My Harley?' he said in disbelief, twisting around to point a finger at the bike. 'Lady, that's not a Harley. That's a Rocket Three.'

With the absurdity of that comment, and of being mown down by a storm in the Arizona desert, Mallory laughed. 'That's a "no", then. Perfect.'

She slung the broken brace on the ground, and dropped her head, defeated. Lightning flashed, but the biker abruptly turned on his heel and strode across the land island towards the interstate.

'What are you doing?' she called as he vaulted the low fence and stepped out onto the road, where traffic raced past at alarming speed. Mallory put her hand over her mouth. Zadie's window lowered again and her face popped out, watching with raised brows.

'Oh shit,' Mallory muttered, as she heard the long squeal of brakes and a blaring horn of a red sedan. The biker stepped aside to give the car room to stop. The driver leaned out his window and yelled through a cloud of blue tyre smoke. Mallory heard the 'Are you crazy?' even over the wind.

The biker didn't seem to care. Mallory had no idea what he said to the driver, but the next moment the car had pulled away, performed the same illegal turn and parked near the Rocket. The driver popped the boot.

'Thanks so much,' Mallory called apologetically to the driver, a middle-aged man in worn jeans and a flannel shirt, with curling brown hair sticking out from under his cap, which he kept adjusting as he helplessly looked on.

In less than a minute, the biker had the stuck nut off the wheel with the borrowed brace and the car fully jacked, as though tyre changing just might be his Olympic sport.

Zadie peered down at him from the window. Mallory, with new hope of beating the storm, was determined to be useful and was ready with the spare. Thunder rolled over them like surf crashing on a beach.

The biker accepted the tyre with one broad hand. 'Had to be a space saver,' was all he muttered as he lowered the jack, job done like a pro. He returned the brace to the accosted driver, who took off at speed. Mallory, still attempting to recover her pride, tried to heft the flat into the boot. She couldn't even lift it. A warm hand touched her back.

'Here,' the man said. 'Let me wrangle that.'

His voice was just like the thunder, and he picked up the tyre as easily as a pool toy. The rain-spotted luggage followed.

Embarrassed, Mallory couldn't quite meet his eyes. Jock was the one who stepped up.

'Thanks, mate,' he said, offering the man his hand.

Ernie wound down his window. 'Are we ready now?'

The biker was unhurriedly wiping his hands on a blue cloth he must have pulled from his pocket, and his eyes finally caught Mallory's. 'Your grandparents?' he asked.

'Not exactly,' she said quickly, wanting to transform into something small and furry that could dart off to hide under the swaying grass.

A smile curved his lips. 'Not from around here, are you? Not with an accent like that. Australian?'

All Mallory could do was look at the ground. 'Guess so.'

'Well, Miss Australia, Winslow's still twenty clicks down the road,' he said, shoving the cloth back in his pocket. 'You fixin' to stay? Storm's gunna be a bad one and y'all be lucky to beat it now. Y'all can follow me in.'

So that's what she did. They'd only been moving for a minute when the first front hit. The rain came down in drenching sheets, and Mallory had to slow to a crawl just to see the lines ahead of her, often losing sight of the black bike. The knuckles of her uninjured hand were white against the wheel, and her heart thumped a pulse in the injured one. *Please, don't let it hail. Please don't get lost. Don't roll off the road into a flooded ditch.*

Every time lightning flashed through the glass and the thunder boomed, she had to bite her lip and remind herself that she was a grown adult.

Eventually, the downpour eased and they picked up speed, but it never stopped. After twenty-five minutes, the biker indicated a right exit off the highway. After two quick turns, he pulled under a motel awning, the carpark and street swimming.

Mallory took a long minute to peel herself out of the driver's seat and exit the car. The rain rushed down the gutters in torrents. Several guests were standing under the shelter, just watching. The huge black motorbike leaned on its stand, dripping water into a vast puddle, with no sign of the rider.

Ernie limped inside to sort out rooms, so Mallory helped Zadie out of the car.

'Wait,' she said, as Mallory went to lead her inside.

'What?'

Zadie closed her eyes and turned her face towards the storm, and Mallory realised she was enjoying the cold spray drifting in on the wind. Mallory stood with her, feeling those tiny pieces of the storm, and her anxiety finally emptied out.

She could notice other details, then. Jock staring at a sandy mud puddle forming on the footpath, his mind seemingly far away. The gutters overflowing into silver water ribbons from the roof of a derelict-looking KFC next door.

'It rained like this the day we left Nashville. Water drummin' down on the windshield, and all the fields green and muddy,' Zadie said, then glanced at Mallory, her focus a little off. 'But then, you've never seen it.'

Mallory didn't have the chance to respond before Ernie limped out with two keys, explaining that they only had two rooms and she and Jock would have to share. Mallory couldn't have cared less. By the time she was helping Zadie to the toilet, she was shaking from exhaustion and her stomach was rumbling. None of them had had any lunch.

'I'll go and find where we can get some food,' she said wearily.

'The desk said there's shops across the road,' Ernie said, confiscating the keys and meting out some cash. 'Bring back the receipt. The desk will probably lend you an umbrella.' He paused. 'And maybe you should clean up first.'

Only when she made it back to the room she'd be sharing with Jock did she notice the grease smear across her cheek. Her nails were black crescents, and her knuckle skin was bruising blue and purple under the dirt. She washed up quickly and then trekked through the rain with the borrowed umbrella to fetch sandwiches and instant noodles. Once Ernie, Zadie and Jock were eating together, with Ernie refusing all offers of help, she excused herself and put the 'do not disturb' up on the door.

•

Sitting on the bed ten minutes later, she stared at Skype on her phone. She'd already tried to call Duncan twice. The air in this room smelled rather strongly of smoke and something floral, which added to the claustrophobia of the drumming rain, and her feelings of hopeless inadequacy. She knew she should try to sleep, but she was too wired.

Instead, she went back over the bookmarked articles she'd found about Duncan and his company. The words were soon blurring together. His company was on the rise, blah blah, promising future, blah blah. Contracts in the works. Nothing new. She flicked back to his Twitter feed. Since she last looked, he'd posted a handful of new links. Most were interviews with CEOs or business policy articles that made her yawn so hard her jaw cracked. But the last was a list of nominees for an award run by something called the April Roundtable. Unusually, Duncan had commented on his re-tweet: 'So honoured to be in fine company.'

Mallory read through the piece: Duncan was one of five shortlisted up-and-coming CEOs for a grant and some kind of mentorship from 'some of the country's most successful executives'. The article spent most of its copy talking up the innovative approach of Duncan's software, and had a very clichéd quote from Duncan that winning the award would be a 'dream come true'. Mallory snorted. Duncan's dreams had already come true. How many more did he need?

With angry fingers, she stabbed at the email app on her phone. Bridget had sent a message: *I keep getting your voicemail. Are you ok? How far have you driven?* Mallory replied that she was in Arizona, and that she was fine, she just had a new SIM card. She would try to find out the number. She didn't have the energy to relay the details of tyres and storms.

She had just hit send when, unexpectedly, a Skype call came through, Duncan and Harry's picture lighting the screen.

'Hi, baby!' Mallory's heart leapt with joy as Harry resolved in the chair. He'd had a haircut, the sides and back sculpted into crisp lines, so different from the shaggy head he'd gone away with. She saw someone else leaning in behind him, but it wasn't Duncan: it was a woman with brown hair tucked up behind her head, dark eyes, and a nurse-like bearing.

'Ah,' said the woman. 'It's working, Harry. You talk now, go, go.'

'Mummy!' Harry said, his smile broad and happy.

Tears sprang into Mallory's eyes. She wanted to fling her arms around him. 'Oh, I so wanted to talk to you,' she cried. 'Whatcha doing?'

'We're going to the park soon,' he said. 'And we're having pizza tonight and bagels before school tomorrow. And Brady has a pet spider. It's huge, Mummy.'

'Wow,' she said, but all she heard was, *school tomorrow*. Pizza. Bagels. The new haircut. As if this new life was already cemented, the one Duncan had made for him. All fresh and clean and hopeful, while Mallory sat here with the smell of metallic grease clinging to her skin. She had to concentrate to hold herself together as Harry elaborated on the plans and wondered what a pet spider would be like.

'It all sounds fun,' she said carefully, when he finished. 'Are you feeling okay?' She desperately wanted to know.

'I'm good,' he said, then paused, looking down. 'I miss you, Mummy.'

Mallory could hardly speak. 'I miss you, too, Harry. So much. But you can call me anytime, okay? And I'm coming to see you.'

'You are?' He brightened. 'Daddy said you were too busy to talk.'

Mallory bit down hard on her tongue. 'Where's Daddy now?'

'At work. We're going to the park when he comes home.'

'Is that Maria with you?'

The older woman bent down and waved. 'Hello,' she said.

'Thank you so much,' Mallory said. 'I really wanted to talk to Harry.'

The woman glanced up, as if checking the door. She lowered her voice. 'Of course. All boys need their mother. We keep this call our little secret, okay, Harry?'

He nodded fervently. 'Because Daddy says I'm not allowed in his office without him.'

Both she and Maria knew it wasn't the office that was the problem. Mallory blessed the housekeeper for her daring, as Maria stood sentry while Mallory recited *The Little Yellow Digger* for Harry from memory. Finally, Maria said they should go.

After Harry said goodbye and got down, Maria turned back to the screen. 'You said you are coming?' she asked.

'Yes. I've just been delayed because of this volcano thing. I have a long drive left. A few days.'

'Good. Come soon. He misses you. I will try to find another time to call.'

Mallory held on to this hope, though her voice trembled. 'Tell Harry I love him.'

When the Skype screen closed, Mallory let her phone fall to the bed, tears running down her face. Something about that call had punctured her soul. She had to get away for a bit: Jock would want the room soon, and she didn't want to answer questions about her swollen eyes.

She pulled open the door and turned down the long hallway, heading for the little foyer space inside the motel's back door. The rain was still drumming down, but at least she could see outside. Maybe she could stand under the awning in the fresh air.

But someone was already in the foyer, sitting against the wall with his long legs stretched out, his clothes soaked to the skin.

Chapter 8

MALLORY HESITATED. THE BIKER HAD REMOVED HIS JACKET, leaving his sodden black t-shirt to show off muscular arms and a wide chest. That should have been enough for her to turn around, but between his knees sat a king-size bucket of fried chicken. The sight was odd enough for her to pause.

Not that she wanted to speak to him. She didn't want to speak to anyone, not with her red eyes and thoughts of Harry bashing around in her head like moths blinded by a flame.

He looked up and caught her staring. Mallory wanted to die with how much of an idiot she felt. She knew he deserved a thankyou. A short, brief thankyou, and then she would be absolved from his debt. She could walk in the other direction and find her fresh air somewhere else.

She drew herself up and approached, hugging the wall. God, he was a big man, even sitting down. He was tearing into a drumstick with his teeth. Fee-fi-fo-fum, she thought, and almost giggled. Finding the funny helped with the nerves, and anyway, he was a bit too good-looking for a giant.

His hair was standing up in little wet clumps, and she realised from a dark halo on the carpet that his jeans were soaked, too. But the smell of fried chicken was so good she could almost understand why he hadn't changed. Her own stomach rumbled. 'I want to thank you for helping us out,' she said briskly as those blue eyes met hers. 'You didn't have to stop, or to come back for us. It was . . . nice, of you,' she finished. There, that would do.

Awkwardly, she awaited a reply, wondering if he was giving her the silent treatment. Then he swallowed, and she realised he'd been avoiding talking with his mouth full.

'And here I figured you weren't real keen to talk to me,' he said. 'But you're welcome.'

'It's not that,' she said hastily, not wanting to appear rude or ungrateful. 'It's just that you . . .'

'Scared you?'

'No,' she said, too quickly. No way would she admit to that.

A smile curved his lips. 'Infringed on your sense of autonomy by offering to help you change a tyre?' The words rolled carefully – almost hypnotically – off his tongue. Mallory frowned. Wait . . . was he mocking her? Prepared to be annoyed, she searched his face, but his eyes beneath that awful bruise only held a touch of sympathy.

'Well,' she said. 'Maybe a little.'

'Figured. I've got sisters,' he said. He picked up the bucket with his clean hand. 'Want some?'

Oh, she did. After all the rain, and the stress, she couldn't imagine anything better than a big piece of fried chicken. She edged closer.

'The KFC next door looked closed.'

'It is,' he said. 'Bein' repurposed. But the guy at the counter pointed me to another place that does chicken fried steak. Seems they bought up the old containers. Tastes reasonable.'

'Chicken fried steak?'

'Yeah. You know, steak that's fried like chicken,' he added, when she frowned.

'So that's steak?' Mallory said, still confused, but at least she felt less like crying.

He held up the drumstick, pretending to examine it. 'I'm gonna reasonably assume this is chicken. Damn weird-lookin' steak.'

'I'm so confused right now.' Mallory laughed, but she couldn't quite bring herself to sit down. Something about him was just so intimidating. She stood at the door, pretending to look out into the rain.

'Tell you what,' he said, 'I'm just going to sit here real quiet and listen to the rain. You wanna eat something? You go right ahead.'

He bent one leg so he could rest his arm. Mallory knew she either had to leave or take him up on the offer. Finally, she circled, sat two feet away, and peered into the bucket.

He tipped it towards her, shook it invitingly. She selected a wing.

He snorted. 'That's your choice?'

'What?'

'A wing? The runt of the box. At least take a thigh, or a rib, something with actual meat.'

'I like the runt of the box,' she objected, finding it surprisingly easy to push back against his relaxed manner. 'It's got the highest skin to meat ratio, and the skin is the best part.'

'All right,' he said slowly. 'I'll give you that one.'

They ate in silence for a few minutes, Mallory casting glances at him, slowly making him into a real human, and not a bully boy at her mother's door or a killer in a movie.

'You know you're soaked through,' she said finally, feeling comfortable enough to state the obvious.

'What?' he said, looking down at himself. 'Well, strike me dumb, I do believe you're right.'

She made a face. He was definitely mocking her now.

He gave her a sly smile and said, 'Believe me, I know.'

'Why didn't you change? You know the carpet's all wet under you.'

'What are you, my mother?'

She shrugged, and plucked a piece of tender meat from her wing. It tasted as good as it smelled. 'Eat your chicken,' she said.

He laughed. 'Gotta work on that accent, Miss Australia,' he said, pushing his Texas twang into cliché. 'Eat your *darn* chicken, AJ, or me and you are gonna mix, you hear?'

'Eat your *darn* chicken,' she repeated. The 'r' came out all wrong, but he laughed anyway. 'Does your mother really sound like that?'

'Nah. My mother's English, and a professor of literature in Austin. She wouldn't be caught dead soundin' like that. My dad's the Texan. Now my grammy? She'd sound like that.'

'Really?'

'We're a real big mixed bag of contradictions, our house. As for the carpet, I'm not changed because everything's soaked. Jeans, boots, bag, socks. That was a real lot of water, made it all the way down to my toothbrush.'

'Oh,' Mallory said, feeling bad for him, but she couldn't help a laugh.

'Oh yeah, you laugh now,' he said, feigning hurt. 'After I come back for your broken-braced ass.'

'I'm sorry, it's not funny. And you didn't have to come back.'

He shrugged those big shoulders. 'Wasn't going to leave a lady and her grandpas stuck out in a storm, even one who doesn't want help. When I didn't see you come past, figured there was a problem. Went back to check it out.'

'That was nice of you. Really.' A few seconds ticked by. Mallory kept eating, and glancing at him, surprised by how easily he made her laugh. 'Um . . . what happened to your face?'

'Well, see, I had this disagreement with another guy's fist,' he said, matter-of-fact. He dropped another set of cleaned bones on the lid and dug for a fresh piece.

'I guess that makes sense,' she said, sounding wary.

He shrugged. 'There's always someone who wants to take a swing at the big guy. Usually, I walk away. Just not this time.'

A silence settled, acknowledging the conversation had reached a too-personal territory. Mallory looked for another piece of chicken but, feeling her fatigue, didn't pick one up. She really should go and check on Ernie, Zadie and Jock, and then see if she could take a nap. But she couldn't make herself stand and be alone again.

'They're not my grandparents,' she said over the rain.

'I do remember you sayin' that.'

She took a heavy breath. 'I'm just helping out. I was stuck in LA with this volcano thing. They're going to Nashville and I'm going to New York, so we made a deal to travel together.'

He paused his eating and turned to look at her. 'You just decided to help some total strangers you met in the airport?'

'Not exactly,' she said, and explained about working at Silky Oaks, and their nurse walking out on them, and meeting by chance in the airport.

He nodded. 'So just moderate strangers, then. Why Nashville?'

'Going to a wedding, apparently. Except Jock. He's going to Virginia.'

'Lot of effort, driving across country just for a wedding.'

Mallory chuckled. 'That's nothing. They had to break out of Silky Oaks first,' she said. 'But don't tell anyone. Ernie's a bit worried about being found out.'

He grinned. 'That a fact? Guess it must mean a lot to them. And what about the vet? He the one going to Virginia?'

Confusion pulled at her forehead. 'Vet?'

'Vet. Veteran. Guy with the hat?'

'Yeah, that's Jock. What makes you think he's a veteran?'

'I was in the Marines for eight years, just got out last June. I can spot a military man.'

Mallory frowned. The idea hadn't occurred to her, but now she remembered all those models of aircraft and tanks in Jock's room. For the first time, she realised she didn't understand at all why he was living at Silky Oaks. He seemed far more able than the other residents. It must be the problem with his back – he might not be able to cope in his own home anymore.

'You got a name, Miss Australia?' the man said suddenly.

'Mallory,' she said. 'And you're AJ?'

'In the flesh.' He offered his hand, as if they'd only just met. After a moment's hesitation, Mallory shook. Despite his wet clothes, his palm was warm and dry, and enveloped hers like an oversized glove. She winced at the pressure.

'My grip ain't that strong,' he said, quickly releasing her. 'You hurt that hand?'

'It's nothing,' she said, tucking it under her leg. 'What's AJ short for? Albert James?'

'No.'

'Alexander Joel?'

'It's just what my friends call me. So you can do the same. Now we've exchanged chicken grease and all.'

She laughed. 'So, are you headed home to Texas? I know that's the next state over.'

'Two states over. And no, I'm headed to Chicago.'

'For a holiday?'

'Nope. Just doing a long ride, the old route sixty-six, all the way from Santa Monica Pier.' But there was a hesitation in his voice, the same one that Jock had had when Mallory asked about what he was going to do in Virginia.

'You take a long break from work or something?'

He shook his head, but hesitated again. 'I haven't worked since I discharged. I was supposed to be starting a bike shop up in LA, but it . . . fell through. So I hit the road.'

'Just you and your non-Harley Rocket. What?' she said, when he broke into a huge grin.

'My non-Harley Rocket, that's a new one.'

'You didn't think I'd remember?'

'Oh, I'm correctin' all kinds of assumptions now,' he said. 'Yeah, me and my Rocket. It's a Triumph. That's my mother's English genes rubbin' off on me. What's in New York?'

'My son,' she said before she could think.

'You gonna hit Broadway and Times Square together?'

'He's five.'

'Ah.' He nodded a few times, chewing, as if mentally calculating. 'So, what'd *he* do?'

'Who?'

'Your man. I mean, otherwise, why are you driving across the country with folks you don't know to see your boy? Sounds like a man problem. I told you, I have sisters.'

Mallory's appetite evaporated as he hit way too close to home. She became all too aware of herself: what was she doing, sitting here in a hallway talking to this man? Laughing at what he said? When she had so far yet to travel.

'Thanks for the chicken,' she said, standing up. 'But I'd better go.'

'I say something wrong?' he said. She could hear the surprise in his voice.

'No. I just have things to do,' she said, trying not to look back as she walked down the hall.

She tried and failed to lie down and sleep, her thoughts alternating between Harry, and AJ sitting there in his wet clothes. When Jock came back after twenty minutes, his hat wet from the rain, she gave up.

AJ was no longer in the back foyer, so Mallory went to the desk to ask which room he was in, and knocked on his door. He opened it wearing only a towel, looking like a bodybuilder who'd just stepped out of the shower. Oh. My. Lord.

'I was just, you know, thinking . . . I mean, that you didn't have . . . I mean, here,' she said, shoving a folded grey t-shirt towards him and trying to find something fascinating about the doorjamb. 'Jock said it's old and he doesn't want it back.' She felt the flush rise up her neck as her words tripped over themselves.

AJ reached out and took the shirt. 'That's a kindness.'

'Least I can do after you helped us out,' she said. Man, her face was on fire now. She tried to be brave and look up at him, but all she found was a pair of beautiful blue eyes staring down from above that incredible body. 'Anyway, I um, enjoy the shirt. Bye.'

Mallory fled back to her room and shut the door, her face incandescent with embarrassment. She slid into the bathroom before Jock, who was watching the cable news, could ask questions. She stared at herself in the mirror, trying to focus on Harry. Thank goodness all the drama was over, and she wouldn't have to see AJ again.

•

The storm beat itself out in the late evening, the sound of falling water replaced with the hiss of all-night trucks cruising down the rain-washed interstate. Jock was already asleep when Mallory returned from helping Ernie and Zadie into bed. The room was dark, but Mallory could have sworn he was still wearing his hat.

She took an age to fall asleep, her thoughts a carousel that rushed around and around, from desperate longing for Harry to the journey ahead, with brief intrusions of AJ in his towel. She almost wished she hadn't taken him that shirt. Maybe he really was some rough-up guy, with that bike and those bruises on his face. Even if he had seemed perfectly normal to talk to. There'd been bruises on his ribs, too. She couldn't believe she'd told him anything about Harry.

She closed her eyes and rolled over with a groan. They hadn't driven as far as they'd meant to, then the whole thing with the storm and the tyre. Her bruised hand had stiffened. It had been more than enough for one day, without mysterious biker men added in.

As she finally drifted to sleep, she prayed for an easier tomorrow, free of mechanical problems and lies from husbands, and dark knights on steel horses. Just let them stay on the road and cover as many miles as they could.

She woke early with thin light streaming in behind the curtains. Jock had already dressed in shorts and a button-down shirt, his hat in place, and was pulling up the bedsheets, smoothing the creases into precise folds, tucking them tight against the mattress. Mallory watched him with one eye open, thinking of what AJ had said about him. He certainly looked like he knew how to make a bed, army-style.

'Mind if I turn on the TV?' he asked, seeing she was awake. 'Just want to catch the headlines. Then I'm out of here. Give you the room to yourself.'

The morning news was still full of the travel chaos. Mallory, dressed in last night's trackpants and t-shirt, threw back the covers just as fervent knocking came at the door. She found Ernie on the stoop, out of breath.

'It's Zadie,' he said.

Mallory ran as though last night's lightning had electrified her whole body. Zadie sat on the edge of her bed, hands braced, her frail shoulders shuddering up and down with each laboured breath.

Mallory's automatic reaction was to hit the emergency button that would bring the nurses, but she wasn't at work now. Sweat gathered between her shoulderblades. Was Zadie having a heart attack? A stroke? Ernie was pacing back and forth, as though he didn't know what to do first.

'Ernie,' Mallory said. *'Ernie.'*

He stopped pacing.

'Have you called an ambulance?'

'Mallory.' Jock stood in the doorway, pointing at a phone held to his ear. 'They're on their way.'

'Okay, good. Ernie,' she said, putting a hand on his arm, 'the ambulance is on its way. What can we do in the meantime?'

'Yes. Yes, all right.' Ernie finally collected himself, easing down on the bed beside Zadie. He tried to feel her pulse but was hampered by his weak leg and arm, which threw off his balance as he held her wrist. 'Stay with me, love,' Mallory heard him say under his breath. 'Please, stay with me.'

The paramedics' arrival brought relief. Mallory was finally able to take stock as they strapped an oxygen mask and ECG dots on Zadie, and asked a flurry of medical history questions. Zadie was already calmer by then. As the medics monitored her ECG, Mallory sank down onto a desk chair for support, wondering what would happen now.

A few minutes later, one of the paramedics came across. 'We can't find any signs of your grandmother having any heart problems. This might just be a panic attack. But we think it's best she be reviewed in hospital.'

He waited, as if asking for permission. Mallory glanced at Ernie, who had Zadie's hand in his as she lay on the stretcher. 'Yes, of course,' Mallory said.

The Little Colorado Medical Centre was only a few minutes away. Once Zadie had been reviewed and settled, Ernie finally left her side and came out of the room. He was pale, his bad leg trembling. Mallory drew him towards a seat in the hallway, afraid he was about to fall.

'How are you doing?' she asked.

'They're not worried. Seems it was a panic attack. It's happened once before, when she's been disoriented. She just seemed so . . . buoyed by this trip and she's usually so settled in the mornings after a rest. I was caught off guard.'

'I mean, how are *you* doing?'

Ernie blew out a long breath and shot Mallory a quick glance. She saw something vulnerable in his eyes. The stiffness seemed to leave him. 'Oh, I'm fine,' he said. 'Nothing to worry about here. Just a little tired.'

'You take such good care of her.'

Ernie looked down at his feet, as if he was considering what to say. Mallory would have put equal money on a profound insight and a scathing rebuke against the hideous carpet pattern. Finally, he shook his head. 'She is the most amazing woman I ever met,' he said. 'Like a shining star. I couldn't believe she wanted to leave home and come all the way back to Australia with me. She left her family here, their farm, with all the animals she loved. That was a big thing for her.'

'I gathered that,' Mallory said, groping for comforting words. 'She seems to have a kind soul.'

'Yes. A big heart. Generous. Selfless. Then she gets this damned disease. And where's the justice in that? After the good she did all her life, and everything else that happened.' He paused. 'I'm sorry if I made some incorrect assumptions about you. I was . . . glad you were there this morning. I couldn't put my thoughts together. Too long retired, I suppose.'

Mallory smiled, a well of gratitude warming her heart, even if Ernie couldn't quite meet her eyes. 'I was glad to be there, too,' she said.

'This trip is for her, you know,' he went on. 'I promised her, and I'll keep that promise if it's the last thing I do. You know—' He paused again, and this time he looked around, as if remembering where he was.

Abruptly, he set his cane and hauled himself up. 'I should go and . . . find her doctor again. It's not like in Australia. They charge you for everything here. Even that ambulance trip will be a bomb.'

'I can do that for you. Why don't you sit and rest and I'll—'

'No,' he said sharply. 'You take a cab back to the motel. Go and be useful. Make sure we're ready to go when they discharge her.'

Mallory closed her mouth. Just when she thought they were getting somewhere the old Ernie had resurfaced. He shuffled a few steps down the hall, then stopped and looked back, as though he might apologise, but he didn't.

Mallory sighed. But she had seen that moment of tenderness in him, and it allowed her to forgive him everything he'd said.

Chapter 9

ON THE WAY BACK TO THE MOTEL, MALLORY FINALLY remembered the tyre, still flat as a pikelet in the boot of the hire car.

'It's sorted,' Jock said, when Mallory flew in panicking, trying to google somewhere in Winslow to take it before Ernie and Zadie were ready to be picked up. Jock was sitting at the narrow desk, still watching the volcano news.

'What? How is it sorted?'

'Took it to a tyre place.'

Mallory frowned. 'What about your back?'

'I mean, AJ took it to a tyre place.'

Mallory felt as if someone had just smacked her in the forehead. 'AJ? The biker guy? But how on earth did he do that?' She laughed. 'That must have been a funny sight, taking a tyre on a bike . . . wait.' She narrowed her eyes at Jock. 'You let him drive the car?'

'Why not?'

'But you went with him, right?'

'Nope.'

Mallory gaped. 'Ernie doesn't even let *me* have the keys alone. What if he'd . . .'

'What?'

'I don't know! Taken off with the car, or run it into a street pole or something.'

'I didn't know when you were coming back. You'd have been worried if I wasn't here. AJ seems a decent bloke. He knows a good mechanic shop. Did you know he's a mechanic? And now the job's done. No harm.'

'Jock, we just met him on the side of the road. He's not even on the car agreement.'

Jock shrugged. 'Neither are you.'

Mallory threw up her hands. She couldn't argue with that and there were no Rocket motorbikes in the motel carpark, so AJ must already be gone.

They were back on the I-40 by eleven, Ernie impatient and insisting on examining how the suitcases had been loaded before they could leave the hospital. Then they were heading east into the tan grasslands shadowing the Little Colorado River. The only evidence of yesterday's storm was the rapidly evaporating puddles in the low spots on the road verge. By the time they had passed through Holbrook and had swung north, heading for the New Mexico border, the land was dry again. Dust devils twisted across the plains.

Ernie and Zadie slept in the back, unsurprising after the morning's events. Mallory was reminded of Harry as a baby, falling asleep in the chugging Corolla as they drove home from grocery shopping on Saturday mornings. She'd often been coming off an overnight respite centre shift, but even on the nights she hadn't slept much, those small trips had been cherished time with Harry, carrying him on her chest around the supermarket. Duncan had stayed at home, madly coding in the rare time alone, and equally exhausted. How they had all survived those early years was a mystery, but she no longer remembered the exhaustion, only how soft Harry's hair had been against her lips.

The thought tied her stomach in a longing knot, and she sighed, a big gush of air, trying to release the tension.

Jock glanced across from the passenger seat. 'That's a wicked bruise you've got on your hand. You do that yesterday?'

'Oh, yeah. It's nothing. Just my memento of the trip.' In actual fact, Mallory was constantly reminded of it every time she knocked the injury into things.

After a long pause, Jock said, 'I know Ernie's a difficult character to like.'

'Careful, he might hear you,' she said, and glanced in the rear-view.

'Nah, he's out. Last month, I took out the piano accordion when he was asleep like that. Never even moved. The staff on the other hand . . . they moved pretty quick.'

'Let me guess – they didn't want you to disturb anyone?'

He tapped his nose. 'I offered to take it down the garden, or switch to the bagpipes, their choice. I don't think anyone found it funny. It's a stern mob in our wing.'

Mallory laughed, but she felt bad for Jock, too. 'That's a shame. You should be able to play.'

'Maybe they have enough to do. More than one of them's refused to deal with Ernie, and mysteriously transferred somewhere else. Fiona didn't even last a day . . . actually, it was negative time, if you account for the date line. Rate you're going, you're setting a record. That's why he keeps the car keys. Afraid you'll bugger off, too.'

'He does have a knack for being . . . difficult. And opinionated.'

'Yeah,' Jock said, nodding. 'That he does. Bit surprised he's gone his whole life without someone breaking that nose of his. Nutter Butter?'

He offered a packet full of dusty-looking biscuits. Mallory took one and bit down on something crunchy and peanut buttery. She wasn't sure if she liked it.

She chewed meditatively. 'So how is it you're friends?'

'I was in my "try something new" phase.'

Mallory laughed. 'Seriously.'

'Because he's always interesting company. Silky Oaks was a logical move for me, but it can be lonely as hell. He's smart as razors. Always have a good yarn with him. Keeps the old black dog away.'

This time, Jock glanced in the rear-view, then reached around and poked Ernie in the kneecap. 'Hey, Ernie,' he said. When he received no response, he lowered his voice. 'See? Out like a light. The thing is, I can't imagine he was always like this. Must absolutely gall him that he can't work anymore after his stroke. And now he feels like he's losing his wife, too. I think that's why he's like he is.'

Mallory grunted, remembering the vulnerability she'd seen that morning. 'I can understand that.' She fixed her gaze back on the highway, watching it slide under the bonnet. Metre after metre, mile after mile. 'It must have been a huge change.'

'I don't know how much someone else can understand the things that really change you,' Jock said quietly. 'The ones that mean you're never the same again. It's always so personal.'

Mallory thought about Harry in that moment. Would this whole situation be something that changed her forever? Would she fail to bring him home? Would it change him forever too? She hated the idea that her little boy, who'd only just started school, would suddenly realise that he couldn't see his mother anymore. No one else would know what that was really like for him.

'Maybe not,' she said finally, trying to steer her mind back to Silky Oaks. 'But we should be able to make better places to live. I had all these ideas.' And she told him about her aspirations to be the Engagement Manager, to bring in animals and new programs that gave everyone a real connection with life. Jock nodded along, making noises of agreement.

'So you organised those kids coming in every fortnight?'

'Yeah, that was me,' she said. 'I read some research that said having animals and children around could literally bring people back to life. You know, because they're unpredictable. Gives you things to talk about and look forward to.'

'Bit like this trip, I suppose.'

Mallory paused. 'Yes, I guess. Except with fewer volcanoes and flat tyres.'

Jock laughed.

'Ernie said this trip was for Zadie, a promise he made. Do you know what that's about?'

'Not exactly. They're very close, those two,' he said. 'He's protective. She's just lovely. On her good days, she'll talk for hours and hours about her animals and her work. Other days, she'll tell me the same story over and over in the present tense, lost in some childhood memory, or not say much at all.' He shook his head. 'Damn terrible disease, isn't it? That's why I do sudoku.' He held up a book of logic problems, folded back on its spine and scratched with pencil marks. 'Keep the old grey matter firing.'

'Seems to be working,' Mallory said, puzzled about Jock. She couldn't quite reconcile his pleasant, capable persona with him living in a care facility. 'Was it your back that made you move to Silky Oaks?'

'Oh, I have some trouble with a few things. Hard to live in a house when you can't lift a ladder. Nice of that AJ bloke to lend a hand, wasn't it? Nice to see a young fella like that with a good heart.'

'Yes. Nice of him,' she replied, but she didn't want to think about AJ. The memory of him was fading nicely with every mile closer to Harry.

'So, what happened to being the Engagement Manager?' Jock asked.

'Oh. They wanted someone else.'

'I'm sorry.'

Mallory shrugged. 'It's okay. Maybe next time.'

'Or maybe you should work somewhere else.'

Mallory didn't answer. She was too busy thinking about all the things she had to do before work even rated on her priority list.

•

The border crossing into New Mexico was marked only with a small green sign. Ernie and Zadie slept on until Mallory pulled into a truck stop near Gallup. After they lunched on Subway sandwiches, Mallory used the last dollars in her pocket to buy a bag of the cheese-stuffed pretzel things that Jock kept offering her, and another of Nutter Butters.

'Stupid addictive American food,' she muttered as she handed across her money. Great time to become a stress eater.

After that, they were back on the road. Ernie requested a new playlist, so the speakers spilled Buddy Holly and Roy Orbison as they ran neck and neck with the freight trains beside the highway. The landscape gradually greened. Fields appeared beside the road with orderly, tractored rows and trees. Low hills replaced the endless plains, and the highway passed through cuttings of dark fractured rock. They flew over the dry bed of the Rio San Jose, and then on, on, through the rising canyon tops of Albuquerque.

When the sun was sinking, Mallory checked the time and was surprised it was nearly six. They'd been driving for five and a half hours, the GPS indicating they were nearing Santa Rosa.

'Should we stop in the next town or keep going?' she asked, hoping to drive on. The light was still bright and they'd lost time this morning. But it had been a very long day for Zadie.

'Probably best to stop,' Ernie said.

She swung off the I-40 onto the old Route 66 towards downtown Santa Rosa, scanning for a motel. She'd just spotted one on the other side of the road when Zadie gave a strangled cry.

Mallory jumped in fright and reflexively braked, pulling onto the narrow shoulder with a skid. 'What is it?'

Zadie flapped her hands, fumbling with the window buttons, frantically looking behind. 'There!' she said. 'Go back!'

Mallory shot a questioning eyebrow at Ernie, but a passing car blared a horn at them for being half out in the lane, so she pulled out again and kept going.

'No!' Zadie insisted. 'No, no! Go *back*!'

'Turn around,' Ernie said. 'She must have seen something.'

Just barely managing to avoid an accident, Mallory found a place to swing through the centre and head back the way they'd come. Meanwhile, Zadie found the electric window button, wound it down, and took her belt off. That set off some alarm in the car, so Mallory had to stop amid the chaos of Ernie trying to prevent Zadie from hanging out the window and a passing truck blasting a horn at them, and incessant beeping. The car rocked to a halt, Mallory's head and heart pounding. Lord, could she catch a break sometime soon?

'How far back?' Mallory asked, when the window had been wound back up and something like order restored.

Zadie could only point through the rear glass. Mallory made another U-turn and stuck on her hazard lights, driving slowly in the right-hand lane so that other cars could pass. It didn't take long.

'That's it?' Mallory asked, pulling over. Decorating a light pole on the shoulder was a large white poster board with a bucking bronco rider and *Clovis Rodeo* in old-west font.

'You want to go to the rodeo?' Ernie asked.

The joy on Zadie's face said everything. Jock tapped at the GPS. 'Clovis is south of here, near the border with Texas.'

'But that's not where we're going,' Mallory said.

'How far?' Ernie asked.

More tapping. 'Less than two hours.'

A hard belt of steel wrapped around Mallory's resolve. The drive was far enough as it was, the time to reach Harry already insufferably long. 'No,' she said. 'We can't add that time. I need to get to New York, and you said you wanted to reach Nashville as soon as possible. We have to stick to the interstate.'

Zadie's eyes dulled, and she stared forlornly at the sign. Ernie was trying to negotiate. They could find another rodeo to go to after they reached Nashville, couldn't they, Zade? But the atmosphere in the car was thick with disappointment, like when Mallory told Harry he couldn't stop to see a passing train. Zadie wanted to go to *that* rodeo.

Tears built behind Mallory's eyes, and she blinked them away, hopelessly conflicted. How could she believe the things she believed about giving elders more of their lives back, see that excitement in Zadie's face and not make the detour? And yet, how could she be Harry's mother if she did?

Jock let the GPS fall in his lap. 'Look, just pull into that servo up the road. I'll run some calculations. We'll need to make a fuel stop anyway.'

•

Ten minutes later, Mallory leaned on the car with a cold bottle of water pressed to her forehead. She hadn't said a word while helping Ernie or Zadie to the toilet. Zadie was now sitting in the car with the door open, mistakenly thinking they were going to that rodeo. Ernie had spent the past minute trying to convince Mallory.

'You do remember what happened the last two times we left the highway?' Mallory asked, ticking them off on her fingers. 'First, we ended up at the creepy abandoned diner, second, we blew a tyre and were nearly scrubbed out by a storm. Things come in threes.'

'Ridiculous superstition. This won't be like that,' Ernie said. 'Jock, tell her.'

'It doesn't add that much time overall,' Jock said, clearly uncomfortable about being put in the middle. 'Yes, we head south-east, but then we turn across the border after Clovis, and come back to the I-forty at Amarillo. Thirty minutes difference to just staying on the interstate all the way.'

'Plus the time at the rodeo itself.'

'Well, yes, a little of that,' Ernie said. 'What if I make it worth your while, a little bonus cash?'

Mallory closed her eyes on a wave of despair. 'It's not about the money.'

At this, Jock slipped back into the car, ending any stake in the negotiations.

Ernie limped a few steps towards the long shadow cast by the service station's road sign, then turned back. 'Can I have a word in private over here?'

Mallory followed with reluctance. In the shade, she folded her arms. 'It's not that I don't want her to go, Ernie,' she said. 'But I need to be somewhere too.'

He sighed and worked his jaw, as if the words had to be wrangled and forced out of his mouth. She hadn't seen him take such a long time to speak about anything.

'You know, I used to think like that, too,' he said finally. 'All my working life. I always had to be somewhere else.'

Mallory opened her mouth to argue this wasn't about *work*, but he held up a hand, appealing for her patience. His voice became low and full of regret.

'I wasn't a very good husband to her, Mallory. She trusted me, left home for me all those years ago. Moved to a new country where she didn't know anyone. Then I spent our life together working. Always working.'

He paused, then gave a laugh that was more like a startled bray. 'Oh of course it wasn't what I intended to do. I thought when the next stage of my career was done, I'd have more time. When residency was over, when college exams were over. When I moved into private practice. But it never changed. I used to tell her that babies don't respect schedules, and that was why I was always at the hospital. There was always a crisis to sort out. She said she understood.'

He paused again, took a breath, and briefly caught Mallory's eye. Something about him seemed so diminutive under the distant hills. 'Then one day, she's having trouble remembering who I was. And I realised that I wasted all that time with her. I always made her promises – we'll go on this trip, or that trip, but it never happened. I think I broke every promise I ever made her, including the very first one.'

Mallory rubbed her face, moved against her will. This was clearly her cue to ask. 'What was the first one?'

'To get married in the Wightman Chapel in Nashville.'

Mallory looked up. 'So this wedding . . .'

'It's ours,' he said. 'I always believed once was enough, but it's my last chance to make it all up to her, just a little bit, for all the things I promised and never did. She wanted to get married in that chapel, and that's what I'm going to give her.'

Mallory put a hand to her forehead, laughing and shaking her head. 'Here I am, wondering what the next awful thing is that you're going to say to me, and it turns out you're a romantic after all.'

She meant it as a compliment, but Ernie made a sour face and huffed. 'You young people don't know what love is anymore,' he said, but even his grumpiness couldn't dent Mallory's new view of him.

She shook her head. 'I think you're just saying that to make sure I know it's still you in there.'

This time, Ernie smiled and raised a hand, a small gesture, asking for forgiveness, for compassion, to be given all the things that he himself was struggling to give. 'I don't know what's going to happen to us when we return to Australia. I don't know how long she's going to remember me. I would never have done this for me. But since we began, she's said more, remembered more than ever. If she wants to go to a rodeo, I want to take her. I'd like you to help me. Please.'

He set his mouth, as if uttering that last word had been tantamount to spilling his blood all over the Santa Rosa soil.

Mallory tipped her head back and breathed in dust and diesel fumes rolling in off the road. Really, she was helpless in the face of his declaration. And Jock said it wouldn't add much time.

She sighed. 'Better tell Jock to load up the GPS,' she said. 'We don't want to get lost.'

•

They took Highway 84 south. For the first half-hour, the setting sun cut long grey bands across their path, the purple and magenta sky competing with the red earth fields that stained the road a dusky orange. To Mallory, it seemed the twilight would never end, each stretching shadow pushing her further from Harry.

After nearly an hour, the sun was finally gone. They drove through Fort Sumner and the GPS's cheery voice directed them onto Route 60, the road painted in the last pink blush of day.

Mallory stifled a yawn.

'Stop if you see a motel,' Jock said.

'It's only another hour to Clovis.'

'It is. But you're tired. Pull up when you see one.'

'I'm fine, it's not that far.'

'Mal.'

She glanced across. He had a kindness in his eyes. 'Pull over, okay? It's been a long day.'

They spent the night at a Super 8 with rendered block walls and deep green carpet. Jock magicked meals out of the motel reception. Mallory meant to work out the time zones to try Skyping Harry, but the next thing it was eight in the morning and she was lying on the bed with her shoes still on. She hadn't realised how exhausted she was. She flew out of the room in a panic, thinking that Zadie and Ernie must have needed something by now. As it turned out, they were just waking too, so she took care of their showers and toilets.

By the time they'd all eaten breakfast, it was nearly ten, and Mallory's mood was as black as her coffee. The sun was depressingly high as she turned the car east on Route 60. The only thing that buoyed her was Zadie, who had insisted on being dressed in a pair of white jeans, a purple button-down blouse, and a pair of flat-heeled cowboy boots, which were so supple and well-worn they must have been favourites for years.

'She hasn't wanted to wear any of that for ages,' Ernie said with approval. 'I was only hoping when I packed it.'

Such enthusiasm couldn't help but be contagious. Along the hour's drive, the highway cut through tiny, neat towns and joining roads that ran off through golden pastures and were swallowed in the curve of the earth. Fields gradually replaced the pastures, until Mallory drove into the wide streets of Clovis, bustling with horse floats and pick-ups, and good-looking people in jeans and cowboy boots.

When they took a wrong turn, Jock asked directions to the showground from a pair of young cowboys sitting on the tray of their truck, one of them strumming a guitar. Something about the smile the guitar player gave them, and his wishing them a good day and tipping his hat, shot a ray of sunshine into Mallory's mood, and unexpectedly she thought of AJ. It must be the accent.

'Look at that roan,' Zadie said from the back seat, pointing out yet another horse to Ernie. 'Just like Silver Dollar. Lovely mare.'

When they drove into a dusty, grass-studded field that served as the rodeo parking lot, a marshal took one look at the three passengers and directed them to a park near the entrance. As she stepped out of the car, Mallory was swept up into the excitement. Everyone who passed seemed to have a patriotic light burning: American flags adorned bumper stickers and belt buckles, flew on flagpoles and on t-shirts, and were drawn on faces. One horse had red, white and blue ribbons woven in its mane. The air smelled of fresh leather and smoke and turned earth. Competitors passed by with numbers on their backs and tasselled chaps shimmering down their legs.

Then Mallory pulled up short. Standing in the shade of a food stand, being admired by more than a few passers-by, was a shiny and rather unmistakable Rocket motorcycle.

Chapter 10

'DID YOU SEE THAT?' MALLORY ASKED JOCK AS THEY SLOWLY ascended the grandstand stairs.

'What?'

'AJ's Rocket, parked down there.'

'I did,' he said cheerfully. 'Nice ride, that.'

'Do you think he's following us?'

'AJ? Nah, he called to see how we'd gone with the repaired tyre. Mentioned we were going this way. He said it sounded interesting.'

Mallory frowned. 'When did he call?'

'Oh, while you and Ernie were talking at the servo back in Santa Rosa. Gave him my number in Winslow in case we had problems with the tyre.'

'Can we please focus on the task at hand?' Ernie said. 'We don't need to go any higher, Zade.'

Soon, they were seated with a good view of the ring, with several kind people making room on the end of a row. Jock sat on Mallory's left, with Zadie and Ernie to her right.

'I didn't think to bring my hat,' Zadie said, looking wistfully around at the sea of western headgear.

'It would certainly go with that shirt,' Mallory said. 'Though that's the extent of my knowledge. I've got no idea about anything they're doing down there.' She watched as two riders in the ring worked to cut a calf from a pack, and rope it front and back. One rider then jumped down to tie the calf's legs together. Mallory pitied the small helpless animal.

'It's roping,' Zadie said, more lively than Mallory had ever seen her. 'Cowboys started all these games to be faster at their jobs, but I never liked it. Didn't like to see the little calves branded or tied down on the ground like that.'

'No, I imagine not,' Mallory murmured. Down in the ring, the animal was freed quickly, and trotted off seemingly unharmed while the crowd applauded a good time. She found her eye roaming around from time to time, wondering if she would spot AJ. 'What do you like, then?'

Zadie's cheeks plumped. 'Barrell racing.'

They didn't have to wait long to see some. Mallory had to admit it was exciting, the horse and rider flying down the ring, skidding around the three barrels in a clover-leaf pattern before the crowd cheered them home. Zadie sat up straighter, following every round with intense fascination.

'I wish I could still do this,' she said. 'I used to beat my brothers. And oh, how they hated to lose!' She laughed.

Mallory laughed too, and then stopped abruptly as she spotted a tall man in black jeans climbing the stairs. As he rounded the corner, though, she saw it wasn't AJ.

'Fancy some lunch?' Jock said. 'I saw a barbeque downstairs. Want to come, Ern? Got an idea for you. The girls will be all right here for a while.'

'Yes, sit with me,' Zadie said, patting Mallory's knee.

To Mallory's surprise, Ernie went with Jock, the two men taking their time to descend, Ernie feeling for each step with his cane. Mallory's stomach gave a little lurch watching them, like it had every time Harry had wanted to climb somewhere high. Please, she thought, don't let them get lost, or slip on a cow pat and break a hip, or be fleeced by some country scam. She had only vague ideas about what went on at rodeos.

'Does your little boy ride?' Zadie asked, in the next lull between competitors. 'I think you said you had a little boy?' A frown creased her brows.

'Yes,' Mallory said. 'We talked about him in the car. He's five. And no, we don't ride. No horses at the cottage except in storybooks.'

'Oh.' She sounded disappointed. 'What about a dog?'

'No dogs yet,' Mallory said. Harry had started asking for one a year ago, right after Duncan had left. Mallory had resisted because she could only just manage to do everything they needed now. She didn't know how to add another family member into the mix. The chickens didn't count because they mostly looked after themselves. 'He does like our chickens rather a lot, though. He worked out how to pick one up when he was two. I don't know who was more surprised, me or the chicken.'

Zadie chuckled and nodded in approval. 'Sounds like a boy. I was terrified of the rooster in our coop. He was a mean old bird. I steered clear. My brothers would chase him, and he'd chase them right back. One time, he nailed one of them right in the caboose!'

Mallory laughed. 'Bet he was sore after that. Did he learn?'

'Not much. Our house was like a zoo. My brothers were always in scrapes.'

The arena event had now moved on to steer wrestling. Below, a rider burst from the gates at one end of the ring, chasing a steer, then hurled himself onto the animal's neck. Zadie followed the action without a word for three rounds.

'What's your husband do?' she suddenly asked.

Mallory was taken aback and, in her surprise, evaded reality. 'Oh, he's a computer guy. He makes security software. He started the company when he left school and now he, uh, runs it, I guess.'

'And what's he like?'

'He's a good father,' she began, then had to stop because tears threatened to close her throat over. 'He, um, he's dedicated and clever. And he works hard. Long hours.'

She didn't want to talk about this, not while her feelings about Duncan were so muddled, swinging from anger to nostalgia like the needle of a lost compass. In all the reading she'd done, she hadn't come up with an explanation for what he was doing, and that drove her the craziest of all.

'Ernie works long hours,' Zadie said with a gossamer touch of sadness. 'His patients keep him busy.'

Mallory glanced towards the stairs. No sign of Jock or Ernie. 'Does he like his work?' she asked, curious.

'Ernie needs a purpose. He doesn't know what to do at home. Can't sit still a minute before he's lookin' for somethin' to fix, some garden bed to dig up or things of mine to meddle with.'

She chuckled. Mallory cast a sidelong look towards Ernie's empty seat, thinking how difficult a man like that would find life, now that basic balance was a daily problem. 'That sounds practical, but exhausting.'

'Mmm,' agreed Zadie. 'He always says he'll be able to cut back soon. He needs his work, but sometimes you need to just sit. Not run away from your own thoughts. One day it will happen. That will be better for us both, don't you think, Mabel?'

She had a faraway look in her eyes. Mallory squeezed her hand. She wanted to reassure Zadie that Ernie wasn't working anymore, to remind her about the wedding that Ernie said she'd always wanted. But Mallory had a sense that Zadie wasn't in the present moment, so she took a softer approach. 'Will you be seeing your family in Nashville?'

Zadie shook her head slowly. Mallory didn't know if that meant that there wasn't any family to visit, or that they didn't get along.

'What about back home in Australia? Will anyone be worried about you being on this big trip?'

Zadie's focus seemed to return. 'What's there to worry about?'

'I mean, anyone who knows you live at Silky Oaks. Any children?'

'Ernie was always working,' Zadie said again, and Mallory instantly regretted the question. She'd felt safe asking it because Zadie had asked her. Maybe that was why Ernie felt his position so keenly; if they'd wanted children but his career had always come first, it must be a point of sadness.

Zadie turned back to watching the ring, and though the sadness seemed to linger like smoke over the outdoor barbeques, after a few more rounds of horses kicking up dirt and cowboy bravery, Zadie seemed to recover her spirits.

Mallory was grateful. She looked at this woman with her kind eyes and purple shirt, her pictures of her beloved animals, and could only think how cruel it was that age could slowly take her mind. Mallory started thinking about her ideas for animals at Silky Oaks again, and how it could work even if she wasn't the Engagement Manager. Maybe she could start with encouraging the management to accept pets that new residents wanted to bring with them. If she still had a job when all this was over.

Jock and Ernie returned ten minutes later, Jock bearing foil trays of carnival food and a plastic bag of sweating water bottles.

'This looks . . . interesting,' Mallory said, surveying the food.

'You see, what you've got here is all five food groups,' Jock said. 'Meat, grease, starch, gravy and seasoning.'

Mallory shot him a worried look, thinking about Zadie choking, or salt load on old kidneys, or food poisoning putting a vomit-stained delay on the drive.

'There's roast potato, pumpkin and creamy beans in this one,' Jock said, as if he could hear Mallory's thoughts. 'I'm pretty sure those are all vegetables. Is that right, Ernie?'

'Botanically speaking, pumpkin is a fruit,' he said distractedly, as most of his attention was focused on sitting again without falling. He blew out a breath once he was down, and gave Jock a conspiratorial nod. Mallory had never seen him so chipper.

Jock then reached for a bag Mallory hadn't seen, and handed Ernie a crisp white western hat, its brim artfully rolled.

'And this is for you, Zade,' he said.

Zadie's delight could not have been more complete. Mallory swapped seats to allow her and Ernie time together admiring the new hat, and reminiscing about rodeos past, while Mallory and Jock ate. Despite the universally mushed appearance that all takeaway food seemed to absorb from its packaging, it was delicious: soft, smoky barbequed pork, creamy potatoes and beans, sweet pumpkin.

'This is really good,' she said between mouthfuls.

'I know. Find a good food cart, set up forever,' Jock said. 'Zadie's having a good day, too.'

'We had a long chat,' Mallory said, and Zadie was still going. She and Ernie were discussing a high school rodeo association event where she and her brothers had all competed. Something about breakaway roping, and her brothers' team roping and steer wrestling, and two horses named Gravy and Biscuits.

Mallory was surprised when she checked the time and saw two hours had already passed. 'How much longer do you think they'll want to stay?' she asked Jock. 'I was thinking we might start driving again in an hour.'

Jock hesitated, looking guilty. 'About that . . .'

'What now?'

'Ernie's organised with some official downstairs to give Zadie a tour of the yards, and there's a street concert and dance tonight he wants to stay for.'

Mallory put her face in her hands, her fingertips digging into her temples. Why couldn't Ernie just stop to discuss it first? 'We were just supposed to be here a few hours,' she said through her fingers. 'You said it wouldn't set us back much.'

'I know,' Jock said, shifting uncomfortably. 'It does add a day. But to be honest, maybe a rest isn't a bad thing. I was really worried about you driving last night. And the three of us aren't spring chickens. Besides, I don't have the heart to say no when the two of them look like that. Do you?'

Mallory sighed. While she momentarily sympathised with the long-departed Fiona, and fantasised about taking the car and leaving them all here, she knew that they wouldn't be driving on until the morning.

•

The street party was a raucous affair that had spilled out from the showground and into the roads outside. The pavements and footpaths were crowded with jeans, boots and cowboy hats in every shade. Walking back from a drinks stand with bottles of water, Mallory had to take swift evasive action as a teenage girl flew past, her headwear in shocking pink. The hat was the same colour as the fading streaks of the volcanic sunset, which was lending a romantic backdrop to the party. From a temporary stage straddling the tarmac, lilting country music set a smooth celebratory mood.

Still, Mallory found it difficult to relax. While her companions had slept during the afternoon at the motel, she had sat on her bed and googled flights and buses from Nashville to New York, and then the route from LaGuardia to Manhattan. Bridget had emailed again: *I'm thinking of you every hour. Let me know you're safe when you can.* Mallory had written back: *I'm at a rodeo in New Mexico, can you believe it? But tomorrow we'll be across Texas. I'll be in NY in three days.*

After she'd sent the message, she'd stared at the Street View of the front of Duncan's building, burning the image into her mind. Three days, and she would be there. She had to be.

She had meant to sleep, then, but instead she'd returned to puzzling on Duncan himself. Driven by the conversation with Zadie, Mallory had re-read the piece about Duncan being nominated for the April Roundtable award, scouring for clues. Was Harry somehow an advantage to him? The award had been running for over a decade, but aside from announcing winners, there wasn't any history to read about. Mallory typed 'April Roundtable' into Wikipedia. It was a lobby group, working to ensure the government passed pro-business legislation. Mallory snorted. Just Duncan's crowd; he loved to bang on about what the government should or shouldn't be doing for businesses. Mallory had often tuned out, bored to a stupor. With a peal of regret, she wondered if that explained part of why Duncan had walked out: was she just not the right sort of wife for him? She wasn't sophisticated. That had been a secret fear in her heart ever since that disastrous dinner party. But while it still hurt to think he'd rejected her for being herself, it hardly explained his actions with Harry.

She'd fallen asleep worrying at the question, but woken after two hours, surprisingly refreshed; Jock had been right about her needing the rest.

Now, she sat on one of many hay-bale stacks along the footpath, tapping her toes to the music and waiting for Jock to come back from 'checking out the place'. At a nearby table, Ernie and Zadie watched the dancers. The two of them seemed amazingly spry after their own afternoon naps, as though they could keep going until midnight. Zadie had changed her shirt, but the new western hat was still proudly in place. Ernie held Zadie's palm with his strong hand, his head bent towards her, two glasses of sweet tea untouched before them.

Mallory checked the time. Jock had been gone a while. She pretended to watch the dancers. Several girls in short dresses and western boots laughed and twirled on their partners' arms. Mallory gripped her elbows. Ernie and Zadie would be fine for a minute if she went looking for Jock. Better to be doing something than sitting here alone.

She sensed someone staring. She twisted around but no one was behind her except passers-by. On the dancefloor, everyone was intent on their partners. Then she glanced far left across the road, and there was AJ.

He was leaning against an awning post, wearing a cowboy hat. He'd shed his leather jacket, and instead was making art of a pair of blue jeans and a stretched grey shirt. In fact, she may not have recognised him, except that he had such an unmistakable bearing. You couldn't be that tall and not stick out, especially when you were the only man standing still in an ever-moving crowd. His blue eyes held her, a small smile on his lips.

The flush rose up Mallory's neck before she could form a single thought.

He raised a beer bottle in her direction. She gave a half-wave in greeting, then glanced away, rubbing the back of her burning neck. An upbeat song wound to a close, and she clapped with the crowd for something to do. She didn't look back across the street until the opening bars of the next song were flooding from the speakers. He was still there, glancing back from the dancers as if he'd been following her gaze.

He pointed towards the dancers, then gestured across at her, and back at himself. Finally, he raised a palm. The question was clear.

Mallory shook her head. 'No way,' she said, though he couldn't possibly hear her. She was not going to dance. Certainly not with someone she barely knew. Especially with him.

He shrugged philosophically, and Mallory relaxed. She hated dancing. She remembered a boy in her class in high school pestering her to do some lively number at a bush dance. Her face had been incandescent by the end of her long string of refusals, and then he'd called her a bad word under his breath. AJ's straight acceptance of her refusal gave him points in her book. She glanced at him again. He was taking a long draw on the bottle now. Man, he looked good in that hat.

Jock still wasn't back. Maybe she should walk across the street and say hello. But the more she thought about it, the more she wondered what to say – beyond thanks for fixing up the tyre in Winslow – the less her legs would be commanded to move. She sighed, and checked on Ernie and Zadie. Another older couple had sat down at the table, and Ernie was busy gesturing – making introductions, it seemed. They certainly looked like they were having a good time.

Yes, Mallory thought, she would go and say hello. But when she looked back across the road, he was gone. She scanned the footpath. No AJ. And she was suddenly disappointed, as if it was sad to think that glimpse across the street would be the last she ever saw of him.

She stood up and brushed down her shirt more times than it needed, trying to decide whether to turn right, or left and walk all the way around the dancers.

And then someone stepped in beside her, and she smelled soap and spice.

'You reconsidering that dance?' he said.

Mallory looked up at him, at that amused smile on his face, and had to sit down again. 'No. I was just . . . stretching my legs.'

'I see,' he said, and sat down beside her, his weight nearly upsetting the bale. He stretched his legs out. He was still wearing his motorcycle boots, and they reached all the way to the gutter. 'Fancy meeting you here,' he said.

'Still the side of the road, I guess,' she said, looking around the footpath. 'But at least in better circumstances.'

He laughed. 'Yeah. That they are. Beer and everything. You want one?'

Mallory shook her head. 'I'm not much of a drinker. Where on earth did you get that hat?'

AJ put his beer down on the footpath, removed his hat and balanced it on the bottle. 'The Rocket's saddlebags are deep.' He nodded at Ernie's table. 'Whole party still together?'

'I sure hope so,' Mallory said. 'Jock's been gone a while. I'm starting to wonder if I should check on him.'

'You worried?' AJ stretched up to look across the crowd, sounding as though he'd mount a search party if she said she was.

'Not really,' she said. 'At least, not yet.'

'All right, then.' His body relaxed, and he leaned back. 'I never thanked you for the shirt.'

Mallory finally noticed he was wearing Jock's old grey shirt, the one she'd given him in Winslow. Now it was tucked neatly into his jeans, with a belt so thick it looked like it had been cut from a cart harness.

'I didn't recognise it. Looks different on you,' she said.

'I would think.'

'Well,' she said, trying not to marvel at how he made a worn piece of cloth look so reinvigorated – possibly it was the stretching across his biceps. 'Certainly didn't think you'd fit in any of mine.'

He laughed, a low rumble. 'Now there'd be a sight. How's that hand of yours?'

Mallory glanced down at the still-purple bruise. 'Doesn't hurt anymore. Jock told me you had our tyre fixed. Thank you. You didn't have to do that.'

'I had the time. Had to wait for my kit to dry. Your not-grandma was okay then? Jock said she was at the hospital.'

'Zadie. Yeah, she was. She's drinking sweet tea now like it never happened.'

'Southern classic,' AJ said. 'Look, here's trouble.'

Mallory glanced at the table to see Ernie pushing himself up on his cane and drawing Zadie out of her seat. The other couple were already heading towards the dancers. Mallory tensed, ready to leap across and help, but Ernie had managed and was now steering Zadie, very slowly, to the floor.

'Seems she had a panic attack,' Mallory said, watching and praying they wouldn't trip on the kerb or slip on the straw strewn around the tarmac. 'Ernie was keen to leave once they discharged her. I didn't see you at the hotel when we came back.'

'I found a laundromat. You ever seen a duffel bag going round a dryer?'

Mallory laughed, then cleared her throat.

His eyebrows drew together. 'I'm sensing that laugh is about more than my duffel bag.'

'Hard to imagine you in a laundromat,' she said, to avoid

telling him she was battling a flashback of him standing in the motel room door in his towel.

'Why's that?'

'Well, you know,' she gestured up and down his huge frame. 'You're this . . . big, tough guy.'

'And so I can't do laundry? Oh, lady, do you need to see a Marine Corp. First thing you learn after cleaning floors with a toothbrush. You're not a tough guy if you can't harden up and wash your own clothes.'

'Gosh, Bridget would love you,' she said.

AJ's eyebrows tweaked. 'Who's this Bridget?'

'Someone I work with, back home. Never mind.' Mallory smiled, and finally felt her muscles unwinding. While her subconscious might keep reminding her that he looked like a bully, all evidence seemed to suggest otherwise. His physical presence faded after a few minutes talking to him. He seemed so normal. Even charming in his own way. She didn't know what she'd been worried about with him standing across the street. It had been like this last time, too: afraid to talk to him, then finding it easier than she'd imagined. 'I guess I just don't think of a guy like you like that,' she said.

He nodded. 'I know. Like I said last time, you look like me, people tend to make assumptions.'

'When you found us on the highway that first time, do you know what I thought?' she said, feeling the need to confess why she'd behaved so irrationally.

'Now, there's a handsome, mechanically minded man. I should reject his help immediately?'

She laughed. 'Seriously. You reminded me of that movie. About the killer robot? You know, the one with the big guy on the bike? Plus, I hate storms and I wasn't really thinking straight. Maybe you did scare me, a little. Sorry.'

'Hold up.' His eyebrows rose. 'Are you talking about *The Terminator*?'

'That's it!'

One side of his mouth tugged up. 'Great movie,' he said. 'But *The Terminator*'s a cyborg, not a robot.'

'Same, same. Whatever, I don't like horror movies.'

'It's not a horror movie,' he said, in that slow drawl, utterly serious. 'Have you ever actually seen it?'

'Yes, of course. Well, sort of . . .' Her dim memories of that particular movie night were somewhat interrupted by Harry's crying and Duncan's commentary, and at least some time hiding under the blanket. 'Big dude chases some woman across a city, lots of guns and explosions, and she barely gets away at the end?'

She was a little bit proud of how coherent that sounded. AJ shook his head, then tipped his chin towards Ernie and Zadie, who were now doing a shuffling dance in a close hold at the edge of the floor.

'I bet *they* know the plot better than you do. You've got it all backwards.'

'How's that?'

'It's a romance, not a horror story.'

Mallory's incredulous laugh exploded like a firework. 'Yeah, right.'

'For real. Kyle Reese and Sarah Connor.'

'That's the most ridiculous thing I've ever heard.'

'Well, now, seeing as you don't know how to change a tyre, I don't expect you to follow,' AJ said.

'Hey! I know how to change a tyre.'

'That a fact?' he said, grinning.

'I do! At least, when the equipment doesn't decide to *break*,' she muttered.

'I maintain my point. Kyle Reese is a soldier who travels through time for Sarah. But since you haven't really seen it, you wouldn't know.'

'Only you would think that movie is a love story.' Mallory glanced down at his abandoned beer, peeking out from under the hat, and wondered how many he'd had tonight, and how she'd come to be at a New Mexico rodeo, arguing about romance and robots with a leather-wearing biker.

AJ shrugged. 'Soldier volunteers to protect a woman he's never met, but whose picture he's been carrying for years. He has a one-way ticket. He's prepared to die for her. Sounds like true love to me.'

He pressed a hand over his heart in illustration, but Mallory wasn't thinking about the movie, or the rodeo, or anything anymore except the photo of Harry in her own pocket. The slow honky-tonk faded as her stomach curled up. Harry was the one she would die for. What was he doing right now? Was he in bed, asleep already? Eating dinner? Missing her? Was he asking for her, and being told that she was busy? Or did he believe, somewhere in his heart, that she was on her way to find him?

She had to believe that. Especially here in the midst of this rowdy street party, surrounded by people having a good time when she only wanted to be somewhere else. And that made her want to cry, again.

'How about that dance?' she said, standing suddenly. Anything to avoid thinking about the things she could do nothing about right now. The embarrassment of dancing was a lesser evil than crying in front of this man she hardly knew. AJ didn't hesitate except to retrieve his hat, following her to the edge of the floor, where all the women were elaborately twirling to the lively beat.

Mallory stopped short. 'I don't know how to do that,' she said. 'I might not have thought this through. Maybe we should—'

AJ took her hand, and the next second he had moved her into a dance hold. And even though he was so much taller than she was, and she was thrown by the warm feel of his hand on her back, a minute later she was managing to shuffle almost on the beat. 'Nothing to it,' he said. 'You never learned to dance?'

'It wasn't on the Bayside High curriculum,' she said, trying not to stand on his feet. 'I think Ernie and Zadie are more coordinated than me. How is it you know how?'

'A mother obsessed with English Country Dancing . . . and the unfortunate fate of being tall enough to partner my older sisters. Don't ask me about the cotillion. I don't like to talk about it.'

Mallory giggled despite herself, and trod squarely on his foot. 'Sorry! I didn't have any brothers.'

'Don't you worry. These boots can take it. You want to try a turn?'

'I think I might break an ankle,' Mallory hedged, watching a nearby woman neatly spin under her partner's arm, tasselled skirt flying. 'Is that why all the women are wearing boots?'

AJ laughed, and as a long note wound the song to a close, Mallory found herself in a momentary peace. All her problems still existed, but at least she'd wriggled out from under their weight for a few minutes. The next number began with the slow rhythm of a ballad, and AJ drew her closer. Mallory fought the urge to rest her head against his shoulder.

After a few beats just listening to the music, he said, 'You don't really want to be here, do you?'

'What makes you say that?'

'Your face.' He shrugged. 'And circumstances. If you'd had an easier way to New York, I reckon you'd have taken it.'

'Close,' she said softly, and looked away, trying to push the anguish down, counting pale strands of straw to distract herself. It didn't work. She was tired of keeping everything inside.

'He froze my accounts,' she said. 'My husband, I mean. When you guessed it was a man problem, you were right. I landed in LA with the volcano thing happening and I had no money. It was the middle of the night back home and I didn't have anyone I could borrow from. I need to reach New York. This was just what happened.'

'You couldn't charge it?'

'Oh no, I don't have credit cards,' she said quickly. 'People ask me all the time how I cope, but really, it's much easier without.'

He pulled away just a little so he could look at her, in a new and considering way. 'Fancy my sisters could learn a few things . . .' he began, then, 'But this ain't about them.'

'It's my mum, you see,' Mallory rushed out. 'She has this problem. With gambling. She probably has ten credit cards and they're all maxed out. She's always been like that and . . . God, I can't believe I'm telling you this.'

A breeze caught her hair and cooled the back of her burning neck. She was locked in by the understanding in his

147

blue eyes. Now she'd started confessing these things, she'd fallen over a cliff and couldn't stop.

'Growing up in that house,' she went on, 'it was just broken promises, and being afraid to answer the phone or the door because of the debt collectors. Sometimes, they were big guys in leather jackets. I swore I would never let Harry grow up feeling scared like I was. So I don't have credit cards, don't borrow money unless I absolutely have to. I knuckle down and make it all work.'

She shook her head. 'I shouldn't have told you that,' she whispered, feeling exposed, and knowing her face must be bright red. 'God, I'm so embarrassed.'

AJ said nothing for a long minute, but his arm tightened around her. 'That why you don't like horror?'

'I don't know, maybe.' She shrugged. 'I suppose you do?'

'Not my first choice, but in the right mood it feels good to be fake-scared. I've seen worse things in real life than in movies. Except the Japanese ones. Those are messed up.'

'Like *The Grudge* and *Ringu*?'

'Thought you said you didn't like them.'

'Yeah but Duncan does,' she said. 'We had lots of movie nights. Not really my choice, but yeah.'

'Your husband made you watch them anyway?' His accent came out strong.

'Not exactly.' She paused. 'He thought it would be good for me, a kind of therapy. Can't stand storms or horror movies, so I needed hardening up, apparently.'

'How'd that plan work out?'

She dropped her forehead momentarily to his chest, finally laughing in irony. 'Terrible! Still can't stand either one. I'm a hopeless case. He always said I was too much like a mouse.'

AJ's hand moved up, hugging her to him, as if they were more to each other than strangers who'd met on the side of a stormy road. When Mallory raised her head, he looked down on her with a smile. 'Well. I guess the man never saw the mice that hang round a military camp. You don't mess with those critters.'

She laughed again. Somehow, in just that one line, he'd managed to take the sting out of Duncan's long-ago assessment of her. And it felt so good to laugh.

'Even so,' AJ said, 'I kinda miss being on a base.'

'Oh?'

'Yeah. It's like a family there, home away from home. It was my whole adult life until last year. Kinda hard to move on.'

Mallory absorbed the tinge of loss in his eyes, and thought of the new and sometimes bewildered residents at Silky Oaks, who'd left their lives behind, and often not by choice. 'That must be a tough adjustment. But your family will be glad to see you, won't they?'

He paused. 'Actually, I haven't been in touch with them in a while now.'

'No?'

He shook his head.

'You don't get along?'

'Oh, we get along fine.' He was the one looking away now, unable to meet her eyes, and his fingers were moving in a repetitive circle on her lower back. 'It's just been . . . a tough time.'

Mallory guessed, with intuition born of her many years in caring, that something had happened, something more than simply having left his military life behind. Normally, she would not have asked, but here they were dancing together. He was warm against her, his voice a touchstone in the night and the music and everything else in a world spinning around her.

'Has this got anything to do with your bike shop falling through?' she asked. 'That must have been disappointing.'

'Sorta, yeah,' he said, but the slow song was winding up, and he stepped away from her, shutting her down. Across the floor, Ernie led Zadie back to the table. Mallory had a sense of closing time, and she didn't want that, not yet. She wanted to know what had happened. They stood there, facing each other, stuck between dancing and departing, between the intimacy of trusting a new friend and the glossy dismissal you gave to a casual acquaintance.

'You hittin' the road again in the morning?' he asked.

'Yeah,' she said, feeling absurdly miserable. 'You?'

He nodded, and just when it seemed they were about to part as strangers, he smiled at her from under the brim of his hat, and reached out for her hand. Mallory's heart lifted so fast that she reflexively bit her lip, avoiding . . . well, what? To avoid feeling like she was flirting with him?

'You be sure and avoid those service roads,' he said, his smile turning cheeky. All she could think about was how his hand felt around hers.

'We couldn't get two flats on one trip, could we? Fate's not that cruel?'

'Fate's crueller, darlin',' he said, leading her back to the hay bale. He let go of her hand so that he could retrieve the beer bottle and peel the label from the glass. 'You got a pen?'

'Um, I think so.' A habit from her job. She dug in her pocket, and came back with a biro, a freezer marker and a small ball of blue lint. She shook the lint away, embarrassed, and offered the pens. He took the marker, which looked much like a toothpick in his fingers, flipped the label over and wrote on it.

'This is my cell,' he said. 'In case you run into any more problems. You take care now, Mallory.'

His fingers briefly brushed her hand, and then he sauntered away, leaving her staring after him, a twin glow on her skin and in her heart. After a long minute, she went searching for Jock. She found him sitting in a chair not too far away, his back to a shop wall, hat pulled down on his forehead. To Mallory, he seemed wan and downcast.

'Nope, completely fine,' he said, when she asked him about it. 'Probably just walked a bit far. We heading back?'

Chapter 11

THEY DROVE OUT AT SIX-THIRTY THE NEXT MORNING. THE sunrise sky was an oil painting: brilliant red and streaked with long horizon clouds, fading into the last Prussian blue of night.

After the excitement of the rodeo, Zadie seemed a different person. She hummed in the back seat, smoothing the sleeves of a brilliant fuchsia shirt that Mallory had helped her into and, prompted by the passing fields, described the family home she'd grown up in outside Nashville. Rolling green hills, streams that ran through the valleys like showers of crystal, woods where she had wandered with dogs or with Eric the donkey, so tame he didn't need a lead rope.

'Sounds beautiful,' Mallory said. 'Like a fantasy land.'

'Beautiful and magical,' Zadie agreed. 'But hard work, too. We only had a washboard and a wringer to start with. I can remember Mamma stoking up the coal furnace in the basement. And her bringing the big tub outside in summer for me to play in. I always wanted to be outside. Making fairy houses and dreamcatchers in the woods. Even the Bell Witch didn't worry me, though my brothers were scared halfway to Texas.'

Mallory's arms crawled with goosebumps at just the name. She'd seen enough horror movies to fill in the gaps. Jock was the one who asked, 'What's the Bell Witch?'

'Poltergeist,' Zadie said. 'Lives in the woods. But I never saw it.'

'Perhaps we could talk about something else?' Ernie said.

'Yes,' Mallory said quickly, keen to steer well away from poltergeists. 'Let's talk about the rodeo.'

'Real community event, wasn't it?' Ernie said, settling back. 'That's the way that people used to connect with each other. Real, face-to-face conversation. None of this facetweetering rubbish.'

Jock laughed. 'You mean Facebook. And Twitter.'

'Whatever they're called,' Ernie said, waving his good hand dismissively, though he still seemed in fine humour. 'Young people spend far too much time stuck in computers. I never even brought a computer into my practice. You look people in the eye. We got along just fine without computers for as long as I can remember.'

'What about the space program?' Jock said.

'What about it?'

'Well, they had to use computers, and thanks to them we've got this little beauty.' Jock patted the GPS unit. 'Never be lost again.'

Ernie harrumphed. 'Except when it doesn't work.'

'You weren't complaining when I used a computer to book this trip.'

'Maybe not that *you* heard.'

Mallory laughed. Jock shook his head, but he was still smiling.

'I like the net,' he went on. 'You can find out all kinds of interesting things about people. Take Silky Oaks. I know practically who all the visitors are, and most of the staff in our wing. Just look them up online and boom! There's their photo, and a picture of their dog, and their kids, and their resumé. Some of them have their whole profiles visible.'

'How dreadful,' Ernie said.

Mallory snuck a look at Jock. 'Sounds like we need to do some training on privacy settings.'

'Maybe. But it's fun. Mal, back me up on this.'

'Me?' Mallory said.

'Yes. You keep in touch with your friends on Facebook, right?'

Mallory blew out a breath. *Which friends would those be?* 'Actually, not so much. I, um, don't really find it good for keeping in touch with people. My friends from school and I moved pretty far apart, and I see my work friends almost every day. I also don't want to put Harry's pictures up online.'

'Very sensible,' Ernie said.

What Mallory didn't say was that she had no interest in her school friends' pictures of holidays and university graduations, and they would no doubt have no interest in seeing any of Harry. When you were the only person in your class who'd married and had a baby right out of school, everyone else thought you were strange. She was probably the one they had all laughed about when they caught up at cafés on weekends – Mallory, the one who had a baby now and was working to support her nerdy husband who had a pipedream of running a company one day.

Besides, no one who hadn't had children was interested in hearing about the minutiae of daily difficulties – 'sleep deprivation', 'parenting' and 'work/life balance' were highly theoretical concepts for most people under twenty-five. They all seemed to have strong opinions, but no practical experience. Although the online mothers she'd found were worse, having both the strong opinions and the certainty of their own narrow experience to back them up. Mallory had decided to stay away from online communities. She'd learned to ask the older mothers she knew through work any questions, and otherwise she and Duncan had muddled through. The only time she'd felt the urge to drop a boastful post on Facebook was when Duncan's company had finally taken off. She'd been so grateful she hadn't when he'd walked out only weeks later.

'Well, I don't know what I'd do without it,' Jock said, a little more quietly. 'I can talk to other people who paint models. Or find out how to make mashed potatoes taste like they came from a restaurant. You've only been at Silky Oaks six months, Ern, and you've got Zadie. You'll work out how lonely it can get. This time next year you might want to be online, and then you'll find out you have to ask to use the computer room, because the damn thing's locked. Mallory understands, don't you, Mal? She's got plans for Silky Oaks.'

'Oh?' Ernie said, voice swimming with imminent disapproval.

'More aspirations now,' Mallory said hastily. 'I was hoping to be promoted, but it didn't happen.'

'She's the one who organised the kindergarten visits,' Jock said. 'Says the spontaneity is good for people.'

'*You* organised them?' Ernie said.

Mallory sighed. 'Yes. But that will probably be the end of my changes. I had plans to try and have animals – pets – for everyone who wanted one. And gardening, maybe green power programs, an artist in residence, things like that. But I doubt any of it will happen now. Mrs Crawley wasn't impressed.'

'I should think not,' Ernie said severely. 'The costs and the administration must be extraordinary, not to mention the health aspect.'

Mallory pressed her elbows into her sides, feeling as though she was back in the interview room with Mrs Crawley. 'What health aspect?'

'The animal dander and droppings! Not to mention parasites.'

Jock snorted. 'Oh, come on, Ernie. People live with pets every day. What makes us so special we can't have them?'

'It's just not appropriate. It's not appropriate for the class to visit either.'

In the rear-view, Mallory could see Zadie reach a hand to Ernie's knee. Mallory knew she should probably leave this alone when he was so worked up. But she was still smarting after Mrs Crawley's dismissal and her shattered dream.

'Isn't it appropriate to make everyone's life better? This isn't just me making things up. There's research from places overseas that do things differently. Those facilities have lower needs for medication, lower rates of injury and mortality, not to mention the elders are happier. Isn't that appropriate?'

'Elders,' Jock said. 'Oh, I quite like that. Sounds so distinguished.'

'I like it too,' Mallory said quietly. 'But Silky Oaks' policy is that we call everyone "residents", so that's what I do.'

Ernie had said nothing. Finally, he grumbled, 'And where are all these magical overseas places?'

'Here, in the States,' she said. 'And Canada and some other places. I first heard about it on a podcast—'

'That's like the radio, Ern,' Jock said.

'—then I found a lot of information on a website. It's even run by a doctor. They have data and programs and . . . lots of ideas,' she finished, feeling despondent. She really had wanted to see if Silky Oaks could embrace some of those ideas.

She asked Jock to put the radio on, and kept driving. Ernie stared out the window. After two hours, they had left the suburban crush of Amarillo behind and were almost out of the northern wedge of Texas. As they passed the state line into Oklahoma, Mallory stopped briefly to let them all stretch their legs. She sipped on a bottle of water, listening to the rush of the highway. When two motorbikes zoomed past, she wondered if AJ had left Clovis, and whether he had already turned north towards Chicago.

They ate lunch at a truck stop near Clinton. Mallory was cramped from the hours behind the wheel, but their progress on the GPS map was satisfying enough to buoy her spirits, and Jock raided the truck stop's shelves for what he called 'driver sustenance'.

'Don't worry, I got Nutter Butters in there,' he said, and Mallory didn't know whether to thank him for feeding her growing habit. Nothing that addictive could be good for you.

Ernie and Zadie were both dozing within a half-hour. Mallory drummed her fingers on the wheel as they slowed for roadworks. She glanced over at Jock. 'I wouldn't have picked you for google-stalking the visitors at Silky Oaks.'

He gave a small smile. 'They keep the visitor book right there in the open. Easy to find out the names. I'm always glad when people come. Lots of folk there don't have anyone.'

'How about you?'

He shook his head. 'I got an ex-wife, and two kids some-where. They don't really want to know me.'

'I'm so sorry,' she said, surprised.

He shrugged. 'My ex remarried when the kids were little. They call him Dad. It was all a long time ago now.'

There was an uncomfortable pause.

'I've been meaning to ask you about your hat for ages,' Mallory said, trying to redirect. 'Do you fish?'

'Nope, can't say I do.'

'Have you, um, had it a long time?'

'Ages,' he said, tugging on the brim. 'Got it for Christmas one year, and started collecting the badges. Have to keep the bald spot warm, eh?'

He smiled, but too quickly. He clearly didn't want to talk about his hat.

'Did you say your back was the reason you, ah, moved in to Silky Oaks?'

Another pause. 'Partly. I volunteered myself. Wasn't really a good idea to be on my own anymore.'

'But now you're going to see your brother. You excited?'

The length of pause this question prompted was just as uncomfortable as the mention of Jock's estranged family. 'Yes,' he said finally.

'Did he move to the States, or did you move to Australia?'

'We're both originally from upstate New York. Little dairy farm there, near the Finger Lakes.'

'Really? You sound pretty Australian to me.'

'Left when I was young.'

Mallory knew he didn't really want to talk, but she was interested, and keen to help the time pass. 'Did the whole family move, or just you?'

'Just me, I guess. I thought I wanted an adventure.' Jock tipped his head back on the seat rest and gave an audible swallow. The skin over his face was drawn, his mouth turned down, as though he was ill.

'You feeling okay?' she asked.

'A bit queasy.'

'It wasn't something you ate? I wasn't sure about that breakfast.'

Their breakfast had been ambiguous burritos that Jock had organised with the motel, most of which Mallory hadn't eaten.

'Just a little heartburn,' Jock said, pressing a hand over his chest. 'Maybe I should have gone easy on the Red Vines.'

'Do you want me to stop?'

'No, keep driving.' But his shoulders gave a little shiver.

'Too cold?' Mallory reached for the air-conditioning controls which, in line with Ernie's instructions, were blasting frigid streams into the cabin.

Jock waved her away. 'No, it's fine.' He sounded really tired. They cleared the roadworks, and Mallory accelerated.

'How much further do you think we can go today?' she asked after a few minutes.

Silence.

'Jock?'

'Mmm?'

'How much further do you think we can drive today?'

'Oh, right.' He sat up and consulted the GPS, taking a very long time. 'Less than two hours to Oklahoma City,' he said finally.

'That'll only be early afternoon. Where's another three hours after that?'

He tapped away, but it took an age with him pausing to stare out the window. Mallory wondered if the connection was slow. 'Fort Smith, just over the Arkansas border,' he said.

'And how far from there to Nashville?'

Tap, tap, tap. 'Shade over seven hours.'

Seven hours. A day's drive. Mallory let out a breath, her spirits revived. Ahead was smooth road, and the green fields of Oklahoma spread around them to the horizon. The dry landscape of the west had transformed into lush grass and trees. Another day, and she would be done with driving. She could be on a plane or a bus to New York tomorrow night.

'Good,' she said. 'That's good.'

Anticipation fizzed in her blood like bubbles from a shaken soft drink. Tonight, she would ask Ernie for half the money he'd promised and use it to book transport. Between now and then, as the road slipped by, she would think about how good Harry would feel in her arms, and what she would say to Duncan ... What would she say to Duncan?

'There's not much to tell,' Jock said abruptly.

Mallory, deep in simulated conversations, had to wrest her attention back. 'Sorry?'

'About where I'm from. Upstate New York.'

'Oh?'

'It's just like all the clichés.'

'I'm afraid I don't know any,' she said.

Jock shifted in his seat. 'Rolling hills. The Finger Lakes and the Susquehanna River rolling through the valley. White snow in winter, green in spring; red and orange and yellow in autumn. Postcard stuff. And the sunsets . . . even this volcano doesn't have anything on them.'

'Sounds lovely.'

'Yeah, it was. Extreme, too. Winter could be brutal. I can still remember not being able to feel my fingers as I walked down to the milking shed. We used to crack ice off the water troughs.'

'Who's we?'

'Then the summers, they could be so hot the tar on the roads would melt. But it was slow, slower than the cities anyway.'

'Like around Silky Oaks? Growing up on the Bayside felt a long way from the city.'

'Yes. It doesn't have the same scenery, but the pace, yeah.'

Mallory heard movement in the back and glanced at the rear-view. Ernie was rubbing his eyes. 'Where are we?' he asked as Zadie slept on.

'About an hour from Oklahoma City,' Jock answered, and turned towards the window again.

'What are you talking about?' Ernie asked.

'Upstate New York,' Mallory said.

Ernie grunted, like this didn't interest him in the slightest.

'So, how often have you been back?' Mallory asked Jock. From the longing in his voice, it sounded like a place that was in his blood, that he wouldn't allow to go without him for too long.

'Never. Never wanted to before.'

Mallory swallowed her surprise. 'Still have family there?' Something about his description left her with desperate questions.

'Not anymore,' he said.

'Let's stop in Oklahoma City,' Ernie cut in.

'Sure, but just for a rest if everything else is fine,' Mallory said, finding it difficult to leave the conversation with Jock. 'We're going through to Fort Smith for tonight.'

•

Jock never did finish his story. Zadie slept on and on through the rest of the drive, only waking for the afternoon stop. She didn't seem quite herself when they unloaded at the motel, near the heart of Fort Smith, Arkansas. Mallory had to support her elbow all the way from the car to the room, a distance of only five metres that seemed to take an hour. Zadie refused a shower and claimed she wasn't hungry, and so Mallory settled her in an armchair while she brought in the rest of the bags and helped Ernie with the bathroom.

'She might change her mind,' Mallory said, as they finished. 'Must feel better to clean up after the drive.'

'Well, if we'd stopped in O-City like I wanted to,' Ernie began, then cut himself off as if realising that ship had sailed. 'But I suppose we stopped in Clovis. She really enjoyed that, really did.'

'I know,' Mallory said, washing her hands and then pushing the bathroom door open. 'Sounds like she was quite a competitor when she was young.'

'Goes with growing up on a ranch in Tennessee,' Ernie said.

'Did she keep up with that in Australia? I used to see signs for rodeos coming to the riding school when I was a kid.'